William—The Good

also published by
Macmillan Children's Books

Just—William
More William
William Again
William—The Fourth
Still—William
William—The Conqueror
William—The Outlaw
William—In Trouble
William
William—The Bad
William's Happy Days

"DO YOU KNOW WHO I AM?" THE STRANGER SAID MAJESTICALLY.

"NO," SAID WILLIAM SIMPLY. "AN' I BET YOU DON'T KNOW WHO I AM, EITHER."

(See page 41)

William—The Good

RICHMAL CROMPTON

Illustrated by Thomas Henry

MACMILLAN

First published 1928

ISBNs: paperback 0 333 37393 6
hardback 0 333 37387 1

First published in this edition 1984 by

MACMILLAN CHILDREN'S BOOKS
A division of Macmillan Publishers Limited
London and Basingstoke
Associated companies throughout the world

Phototypeset by Wyvern Typesetting Ltd, Bristol
Printed by Richard Clay (The Chaucer Press) Ltd,
Bungay, Suffolk

Contents

An invitation from William

You can join the Outlaws Club!

You will receive

✻ **a special Outlaws wallet containing**

your own Outlaws badge

the Club Rules

and

a letter from William giving you the secret password

To join the Club send a letter with your name and address written in block capitals telling us you want to join the Outlaws, and a postal order for 45p, to

The Outlaws Club
PO Box No 1
Gateshead
NE8 1AJ

You must live in the United Kingdom or the Republic of Ireland in order to join.

Chapter 1

William—The Good

The Christmas holidays had arrived at last and were being celebrated by the Brown family in various ways.

Ethel and her friends were celebrating it by getting up a play which was to be acted before the village on Christmas Eve. Mrs. Brown was celebrating it by having a whist drive, and William was celebrating it by having influenza.

Though William is my hero, I will not pretend that he made a good invalid. On the contrary he made a very bad one. He possessed none of those virtues of patience, forbearance, and resignation necessary to a good invalid. William, suffering from influenza, was in a state of violent rebellion against fate. And he was even worse when the virulence of the attack had waned and he could sit up in bed and partake of nourishment.

There was, he bitterly complained, nothing to do.

Kind friends brought him in jig-saw puzzles, but, as he informed those about him incessantly, he didn't see what people *saw* in jig-saw puzzles. He didn't like doing them and he didn't see any good in them when they were done. As an occupation, they were, he gave his family to understand, beneath his contempt. His family offered him other occupations. One of his aunts kindly sent him a scrap album, and another kindly sent him a book of general knowledge questions. He grew more morose and bitter every day. No, he didn't want to do any of those things. He wanted to get up. Well, why not? Well, to-morrow then? Well, WHY NOT?

Well, he'd always said that the doctor wasn't any use.

He'd said so ever since he wouldn't let him stay in bed when he felt really ill—that day last term when he hadn't done any of his homework. And now, now that it was holidays, he made him stay in bed. He simply couldn't think why they went on having a man like that for a doctor, a man who simply did everything he could to annoy people. That was all the doctoring he knew, doing everything he could to annoy people. It was a wonder they weren't all dead with a doctor like that. No, he didn't want to do cross-word puzzles.

What did he want to do then?

He wanted to get up and go out. He wanted to go and play Red Indians with Ginger and Douglas and Henry. He wanted to go to the old barn and play Lions and Tamers. He wanted to go and be an Outlaw in the woods. That was what he wanted to do. Well, then, if he couldn't do anything he wanted to do what did they keep asking him what he wanted to do for?

In disgust he turned over on his side, took up a book which a great-aunt had sent him the day before and began to read it.

Now it was a book which in ordinary circumstances would not have appealed to William at all. It was a book in the "Ministering Children" tradition with a hero as unlike William as could possibly be imagined. William merely took it up to prove to the whole world how miserably, unutterably bored he was. But he read it. And because he was so bored, the story began to grip him. He read it chapter by chapter, even receiving his mid-morning cup of beef tea without his usual execrations.

It was perhaps because of his weakened condition that the story gripped him. The hero was a boy about William's age, whose angelic character made him the sunshine of his home. He had a beautiful sister who, he discovered, was a secret drinker. He pleaded with her to give up the fatal habit. That was a very beautiful scene. It had, however, little effect upon the sister. She became a thief. The youthful hero saw her steal a valuable piece of old silver in a friend's house. At great risk of being himself suspected of the crime he took it back and replaced it in the friend's house. The sister was so deeply touched by this that she gave up her habits of drink and theft and the story ended with a youthful hero, his halo gleaming more brightly than ever, setting out to rescue other criminals from their lives of crime.

"Gosh!" said William as he closed the book, "an' only eleven, same as me."

At once, William ceased to long to play Red Indians with Ginger and Henry and Douglas. Instead he began to long to rescue those around him from lives of crime.

* * *

Downstairs, Ethel and her mother were talking. "Have you settled the parts for your play yet, dear?" said Mrs. Brown.

"N-no," said Ethel, "it's all rather annoying. Mrs. Hawkins has taken up the whole thing, and is managing everything. Of course, we can't stop her, because, after all, she's going to finance the whole show, and have footlights put up and make it awfully posh, but still—she's insisting on our doing scenes from 'As You Like It'. She *would* want Shakespeare. She's so deadly dull herself."

"And you'll be Rosalind, I suppose?" said Mrs. Brown quite placidly.

Ethel was always the heroine of any play she acted in.

But Ethel's face grew slightly overcast.

"Well," she said, "that's the question. Mrs. Hawkins is having a sort of trial at her house. It lies between me and Dolly Morton and Blanche Jones. She wants to hear us all read the part. She's going to have all the committee at her house on Tuesday to hear us all read the part. It *does* seem rather silly, doesn't it? I mean, making such a fuss about it. However——"

"Well, darling," said Mrs. Brown, "when you are at the Hawkins' I wish you'd ask them if they can let us have one bon-bon dish. I haven't quite enough for all the tables at the whist drive, and Mrs. Hawkins kindly said she'd lend me as many as I liked."

"Very well," said Ethel absently. "I shall feel *mad* if she gives the part to Dolly Morton or Blanche Jones. I've had much more experience and after all——"

After all, Ethel's silence said, she was far and away the prettiest girl in the village. She heaved a sigh.

Mrs. Brown, as if infected with the general melancholy, also heaved a sigh.

"The doctor says that William can get up to-morrow," she said.

Ethel groaned.

"Well," said her mother wearily, "he *can't* be worse up than he's been in bed the last few days."

"Oh, *can't* he?" said Ethel meaningly.

"But he's been quite good this afternoon," admitted Mrs. Brown in a voice almost of awe, "reading a book quietly all the time."

"Then he'll be awful to-morrow," prophesied Ethel, gloomily, and with the suspicion of a nasal intonation.

Mrs. Brown looked at her suspiciously. "You haven't got a cold, have you, Ethel?" she said.

"No," said Ethel hastily.

"Because if you have," said Mrs. Brown, "it's probably influenza, and you must go to bed the minute you feel it coming on."

* * *

William was downstairs. He did not, strangely enough, want to go out and play Red Indians with Henry, Douglas and Ginger. That lassitude which is always the after effect of influenza was heavy upon him. William, however, did not know that this was the cause.

He mistook it for a change of heart. He believed his character to be completely altered. He did not want to be a rough boy ranging over the countryside any longer. He wanted to be a boy wearing a halo and rescuing those around him from lives of crime. He watched Ethel meditatively where she sat on the other side of the room reading a newspaper. She looked irritatingly virtuous.

William found it difficult to imagine her drinking in secret or stealing pieces of silver from a neighbour's drawing-room. It was, he reflected, just his luck to have a sister who was as irritating a sister as could be, and yet who would afford him no opportunity of rescuing her from a life of crime. His expression grew more and more morose as he watched her. There she sat with no thought in her mind but her silly magazine, resolutely refusing either to drink or steal.

As a matter of fact, Ethel had other thoughts in her mind than the magazine upon which she was apparently so intent. Ethel was afraid. There was no doubt at all that a cold was developing in Ethel's head, and Ethel knew that, should her mother guess it, she would be summarily despatched to bed and would not be able to attend Mrs. Hawkins' meeting, and that the result would be that either Dolly Morton or Blanche Jones would be Rosalind in the play.

Now, Ethel had set her heart upon being Rosalind. She felt that she would die of shame if Dolly Morton or Blanche Jones were chosen as Rosalind in her stead. And, therefore, the peculiar feeling of muzziness, the difficulty of enunciating certain consonants that she was at present experiencing, filled her with apprehension. A cold was coming on. There was no doubt of it at all. If only it could escape her mother's notice till after to-day!

After to-day, when she was chosen as Rosalind, Ethel was willing to retire to bed and stay there as long as her mother wanted, but not till then. Hence she was silent and avoided her mother as much as possible. She might, of course, take something to stave it off (though she knew that that was generally impossible), but her mother had the keys of the medicine cupboard, and to ask for anything would arouse suspicion.

The muzziness was growing muzzier every minute, and she had a horrible suspicion that her nose was red.

Suddenly she remembered that when William's cold began, her mother had bought a bottle of "Cold Cure," and given it to him after meals for the first day before the cold changed to influenza and he had to go to bed. She believed that it was still in the sideboard cupboard in the dining-room. She'd sneak it upstairs and take some. It might just stave it off till to-night.

She looked up and met William's earnest gaze. What was he looking at her like that for? He'd probably noticed that she'd got a cold and he'd go and tell her mother. It would be just like him. He'd blurt out, "Mother, Ethel's got a cold," and she'd be packed off to bed and not be able to go to Mrs. Hawkins', and Dolly Morton or Blanche Jones would be Rosalind and she'd die of shame. She stared at him very haughtily, and then went off to the dining-room for the bottle of "Cold Cure."

But her manner had attracted William's attention. He moved his seat so that he could see her through the crack of the door. She went across the hall to the dining-room. She looked about her furtively. She tiptoed to the hall again and looked up and down to make sure that no one saw her. Then very furtively she went back into the dining-room. She opened the sideboard cupboard and with a quick guilty movement took out a bottle and hid it under her jumper. *A bottle!* William gaped. His eyes bulged. *A bottle!* Still looking furtively around her she went upstairs. William followed just as furtively. He heard her bolt her bedroom door. He put his eye to the keyhole and there he saw her raise the bottle to her lips. He was amazed, but he had to believe the evidence of his eyes. She was a secret drinker. Ethel was a secret drinker!

His spirits rose. He must set about the work of reforming her at once. The first thing to do was to plead with her. That in the book had been a very moving and beautiful scene.

* * *

He was waiting for her in the morning-room when she came down. Yes, she did look like a secret drinker now that he came to look at her more particularly. She'd got a red nose. They always had red noses. She threw him a haughty glance, took up her magazine and began to read it. Then suddenly she was shaken by an enormous sneeze. It came upon her unawares, before she could stop it. As a matter of fact, it wasn't the sort of sneeze you could stop. It was the sort that proclaimed to all the world that you have a cold, perhaps influenza, and that you ought to be in bed.

Thank heaven, thought Ethel, her mother was in the village shopping. William, however, was gazing at her

WILLIAM MOVED HIS SEAT SO THAT HE COULD SEE HIS SISTER THROUGH THE CRACK OF THE DOOR.

ETHEL WENT ACROSS THE HALL TO THE DINING-ROOM.
SHE LOOKED ABOUT HER FURTIVELY.

reproachfully. He was, she supposed, wondering bitterly why she was allowed to go about with a cold when he'd been went to bed at once. She gazed at him defiantly. William, as a matter of fact, had not noticed the sneeze at all. His mind was so taken up by the problem of how to plead with her to give up her habit of secret drinking.

He began rather sternly.

"Ethel, I know all about it."

"Whatever do you mean?" said Ethel feebly, "all about it! Why, I'm perfectly all right. *Perfectly* all right. Anyone can do it once. Once is nothing. It—it's *good* for you to do it once."

Of course, she'd say that, thought William. In his book the sister had said that it was the first time —— "Have you only done it once, Ethel?" he said earnestly.

"*Of course*," she snapped, "that was the first time."

She must have known that he'd seen her through the keyhole. He couldn't think what to say next. He'd quite forgotten what the boy in the book had said, but he remembered suddenly Ethel's pride in her personal appearance.

"It's making you look awful," he said.

"It *isn't*," snapped Ethel; "my nose *is* a tiny bit red, but it's not due to that at all."

"I bet it *is*," said William.

"It *isn't*," said Ethel. "Anyway"—and she became almost humble in her pleading—"anyway—you won't say anything to mother about it, will you? Promise."

"Very well," said William.

He promised quite willingly, because he didn't want his mother interfering in it any more than Ethel did. He wanted to have the sole glory of saving Ethel from her life of crime, and if their mother knew, of course, she'd take the whole thing out of his hands.

* * *

"Ethel," said Mrs. Brown tentatively, "I wonder—I'd be so much obliged if you'd take William with you to Mrs. Hawkins'. He's getting so restless indoors, and I daren't let him go out and play, because you know what he is. He'd be walking in the ditch and getting his feet wet and getting pneumonia or something. But if he goes with you it will be a nice little change for him, and you can keep an eye on him, and—well"—vaguely—"it'll be about Shakespeare, and that's improving. His last school report was awful. And, as I say, it will be a nice little change for him."

Ethel knew that her mother was thinking about a nice little change for herself, rather than for William, but, chiefly lest her pronunciation of certain consonants should betray her, she acquiesced.

"Then I can get on with the preparations for the whist drive," said Mrs. Brown, "and you won't forget to ask for the bon-bon dish, will you, dear?"

Ethel said "No" (or rather "Do"), and felt grateful to the whist drive because she knew that it was preoccupation with it that prevented her mother from recognising the symptoms of a cold in the head which were becoming more and more pronounced every minute.

William showed unexpected docility when ordered to accompany Ethel to Mrs. Hawkins'. He felt that he had not so far acquitted himself with any conspicuous success in his rôle of reformer of Ethel. He could not flatter himself that anything he had said would have saved her from drink. He might get another chance during the afternoon.

There was quite a large gathering at Mrs. Hawkins'.

There was Mrs. Hawkins and her daughter Betty. There was the Committee of the Dramatic Society. There were Dolly Morton, brought by Mrs. Morton, and Blanche Jones, brought by Mrs. Jones. They were first of all given tea by Mrs. Hawkins in the morning-room. "And then we'll have our little reading," she added.

She accepted William's presence with resignation and without enthusiasm.

"Of course, dear," she said to Ethel, "I *quite* understand. I know they're trying, especially when they've been ill. Yes, it's a *joy* to have him. You'll be very quiet, won't you, my little man, because this is a very serious occasion. Very serious indeed."

Ethel sat down next to Betty Hawkins, and a great depression stole over her. She knew perfectly well that she could not be chosen as Rosalind in competition with Dolly Morton or Blanche Jones, or indeed with anyone at all.

She was feeling muzzier and muzzier every minute. Her eyes were watery. Her nose was red. She knew that with the best will in the world she was incapable of giving full value to the beauty of Rosalind's lines.

"*I show bore birth than I am bistress of*," she quoted softly to herself, "*and would you yet I were berrier?*"

No, it was quite hopeless. Moreover, Mrs. Morton and Mrs. Jones were both very wealthy, and fairly recently additions to the neighbourhood, and she had a suspicion that Mrs. Hawkins was trying to ingratiate herself with them. Yet she felt that she simply couldn't go on living if she didn't get the part of Rosalind. Mrs. Hawkins handed her a cup of tea. William had wandered away. He had gone over to the bay window where Mrs. Morton sat alone. Mrs. Morton was inclined to be superior and wasn't quite sure whether or no she were compromising herself in any way by allowing herself to be drawn into Mrs. Hawkins' circle. So she sat as far aloof from it as she could. Of course, she wanted Dolly to be chosen as Rosalind. On the other hand, it was never wise to be too friendly with people till you knew exactly where they stood.

William sat down on the window-seat next to her, watching Ethel morosely. Everyone must know that she'd been drinking. Her nose was as red as anything now.

Suddenly, Mrs. Morton said to him:

"Your sister doesn't look very well."

"Oh, she's all right," said William absently. "I mean, she's all right in one way. She's not ill or anything." Then he added casually: "It's only that she drinks."

"*W-what?*" said Mrs. Morton, putting her cup down hastily upon an occasional table, because she felt too unnerved to hold it any longer.

"She drinks," said William more clearly and with a certain irritation at having to repeat himself. "Din't you hear what I said? I said she drinks. She keeps a bottle of it in her room and locks the door an' drinks it. It's that what makes her look like that."

"B-but," gasped Mrs. Morton, "how terrible."

"Yes," asserted William carelessly, "it's terrible all right. She takes it up to her bedroom, in a bottle an' locks the door and drinks it there, an' then comes out lookin' like that."

Mrs. Morton's worst fears were justified. Whatever sort of people had she let herself be drawn among? She rose, summoned her daughter with a regal gesture, and turning to Mrs. Hawkins said with magnificent hauteur:

"I'm sorry, Mrs. Hawkins, but I've just remembered a most important engagement, and I'm afraid I must go at once."

And she swept out, followed by the meek Dolly.

"OH, ETHEL'S NOT ILL OR ANYTHING!" SAID WILLIAM. "IT'S ONLY THAT SHE DRINKS." "W-WHAT?" SAID MRS. MORTON.

Gradually Mrs. Hawkins recovered from her paralysis.

"Well," she gasped, "what simply extraordinary behaviour! I never *heard*—— Well, I wouldn't have her daughter now for Rosalind not for a thousand pounds."

William, left high and dry on his window seat, continued thoughtfully to consume cakes. Perhaps he oughtn't to have told her that. It had seemed to upset her. Well, he wouldn't tell anyone else, though he did rather want people to know about the noble work he was doing in reforming Ethel. What was the use of reforming anyone if people didn't know you were doing it?

"William, dear," said Mrs. Hawkins sweetly, "would you like to go into the dining-room and see if you can find anything you'd like to read on the shelves there?"

William went, and conversation became general.

"Oh, I nearly forgot," said Ethel to Betty Hawkins. "Mother asked me to ask you to lend us a bon-bon dish for the whist drive. We find we won't have *quite* enough after all."

"Oh, rather. I'll get one for you."

"Don't bother. Tell me where to get it."

"Well, there's one on the silver table in the drawing-room. I'll get it and wrap it up for you."

"No, don't bother. I can slip it into my bag. I can get out much more easily than you can."

Thus it was that William, returning from the dining-room to inform the company that he hadn't been able to find anything interesting to read, was met by the sight of his sister creeping out of the morning-room where everyone was assembled and going alone into the empty drawing-room.

William glued his eye to the crack in the door and watched her.

She took a piece of silver from a table and slipped it into her hand-bag and then returned to the drawing-room, without noticing him. He stood for a minute motionless, amazed. Crumbs! *Crumbs!* She was like the girl in the book. She stole as well as being a secret drinker. He must do something at once. He must get the thing she'd stolen and put it back in its place again. That was what the boy in the book had done.

He returned to the morning-room. They hadn't begun the trial reading yet: they were all talking at once. They were discussing recent social happenings in the village. Mrs. Jones, as a newcomer, was feeling slightly out of it, and Mrs. Jones had a lively sense of her own importance and did not like feeling out of it. She had previously, of course, been kept in countenance by Mrs. Morton, and she was still wondering what had made Mrs. Morton go off like that. But there was no doubt at all that people weren't making enough fuss of her, so she rose and said with an air of great dignity:

"Mrs. Hawkins, I am suffering from a headache. May I go into your drawing-room and lie down?"

She had often found that that focused the attention of everyone upon her. It did in this instance. They all leapt to their feet solicitously, fussed about her, escorted her to the drawing-room, drew down the blinds and left her well pleased with the stir she had made.

This, she thought, ought to assure the part of Rosalind for Blanche. They wouldn't surely risk making her headache worse by giving the part to anyone else. Meanwhile, William was seated upon the floor between Betty Hawkins and Ethel. His whole attention was focused upon Ethel's bag which she had carelessly deposited upon the floor. Very slowly, very furtively, inch by inch, William was drawing it towards him. At last he was able to draw it behind him. No one had seen. Betty and Ethel were talking about the play.

"Do, I don't really bind what I ab," Ethel was saying, untruthfully.

Very skilfully, William took the silver dish out of the bag, slipped it into his pocket and put back the bag where it had been before. Then, murmuring something about going to look at the books again, he slipped from the room and went back to the drawing-room to replace it. He had quite forgotten Mrs. Jones, but just as he was furtively replacing the dish upon the table, her stern, accusing voice came from the dark corner of the room where the couch stood.

"What are you doing, boy?"

William jumped violently.

"I—I—I'm putting this back," he explained.

"What did you take it away for?" said Mrs. Jones still more sternly. William hastened to excuse himself.

"I din' take it," he said. "Ethel took it," then, hastening to excuse Ethel. "She—she sort of can't help taking things. I always," he added virtuously, "try'n put back the things she's took."

Mrs. Jones raised herself, tall and dignified, from her couch.

"Do you mean to say," she said, "that your sister *stole* it."

"Yes," said William. "She does steal things. We always try'n put them back when we find things she's stole. I found this just now in her bag."

"A kleptomaniac," exclaimed Mrs. Jones, "and I am expected to allow my daughter to associate with such people!"

Quivering with indignation, she returned to the morning-room. William followed her.

"Feeling better?" said Mrs. Hawkins brightly, "because if you are, I think we might begin the reading."

"I find," said Mrs. Jones icily, "that I cannot, after all, stay for the reading. I must be getting home at once. Come, Blanche!"

When she'd gone, Mrs. Hawkins looked about her in helpless amazement.

"Isn't it *extraordinary?*" she said. "I simply can't understand it. It's an absolute mystery to me what's come over them. Now, have I said a single thing that could have annoyed them?"

They assured her that she hadn't.

"Well," she said, "it's just as well to have no dealings with people as unaccountable as that, so, Ethel dear, you'd better take Rosalind after all."

"Thag you so buch," said Ethel gratefully.

"You've got a little cold, haven't you?"

"Yes, I hab," admitted Ethel, "perhaps I'd better go hobe dow. Bother asked me to ask you kidly to led her a bod-bod dish as Betty kidly let me hab this frob the drawing-roob."

She opened her bag.

"It's god," she gasped.

William was looking very inscrutable, but his mind was working hard. There was more in this, he decided, than had met his eye.

Betty had gone into the drawing-room and now returned with the bon-bon dish.

"You never took it," she said.

"But I did," persisted Ethel. "I dow I did. It's bost bysterious."

"You'd better get home to bed, my dear," said Mrs. Hawkins.

"Yes. I'm *awfully* glad I'b goig to be Rosalid. Cub od, Williab."

William did not speak till they'd reached the road. Then he said slowly:

"She'd *lent* you that silver thing Ethel?"

"Of course," said Ethel shortly.

"An—an' you've—you've got a bad cold?" he continued.

Ethel did not consider this worth an answer, so they walked on in silence.

"Well, dear?" said Mrs. Brown when they reached home.

"I'b goig to be Rosalid," said Ethel, "but I've got a bit of co'd, so I think I'll go to bed." In her relief at having been chosen as Rosalind, she became expansive and confidential. "I knew I'd god a co'd this borning, an' I sneaked up that boddle of co'd cure ad drank sobe id my bed roob, but it didn't do any good."

William blinked.

"Was it—was it the cold cure stuff you were drinkin' in your room, Ethel?"

"You'd better go to bed, too, William," said his mother. "The doctor said that you were to go to bed early this week."

"All right," said William with unexpected meakness. "I don't mind going to bed."

Still looking very thoughtful, William went to bed.

"Was he all right at Mrs. Hawkins?" said his mother anxiously to Ethel.

"Oh, yes," said Ethel, "he was quite good."

"I'm so glad," said Mrs. Brown, relieved, "because you know he sometimes does such extraordinary things when he goes out."

"Oh, no," said Ethel, preparing to follow William up to bed, "he was quite all right." She was silent for a minute, as she remembered the abrupt departures of Mrs. Morton and Mrs. Jones, and the mysterious disappearance of the bon-bon dish from her bag.

"Sobe rather fuddy things did happed," she said, "but Williab couldn't possibly have beed respodsible for any of theb."

Chapter 2

William—The Great Actor

It was announced in the village that the Literary Society was going to give a play on Christmas Eve. It was a tradition that a play should be given in the village every Christmas Eve. It did not much matter who gave it or what it was about or what it was in aid of, but the village had begun to expect a play of some sort on Christmas Eve. William's sister Ethel and her friends had at first decided to do scenes from "As You Like It," but this had fallen through partly because Ethel had succumbed to influenza as soon as the cast was arranged, and partly because of other complications too involved to enter into.

So the Literary Society had stepped into the breach, and had announced that it was going to act a play in aid of its Cinematograph Fund. The Literary Society was trying to collect enough money to buy a cinematograph. Cinematographs, the President said, were so educational. But that was not the only reason. Membership of the Literary Society had lately begun to fall alarmingly, chiefly because, as everyone freely admitted, the meetings were so dull. They had heard Miss Greene-Joanes read her paper on "The Influence of Browning" five times, and they had had the Debate on "That the

Romantic School has contributed more to Literature than the Classical School" three times, and they'd had a Sale of Work and a Treasure Hunt and a picnic and there didn't seem to be anything else to do in the literary line. Mrs. Bruce Monkton-Bruce, the Secretary, said that it wasn't her fault. She'd written to ask Bernard Shaw, Arnold Bennett, E. Einstein, M. Coué and H. G. Wells to come down to address them and it wasn't her fault that they hadn't answered. She'd enclosed a stamped addressed envelope in each case. More than once they'd tried reading Shakespeare aloud, but it only seemed to send the members to sleep and then they woke up cross.

But the suggestion of the cinematograph had put fresh life into the Society. There had been nearly six new members (the sixth hadn't quite made up her mind) since the idea was first mooted. The more earnest ones had dreams of watching improving films, such as those depicting Sunrise on the Alps or the Life of a Kidney Bean from the cradle to the grave, while the less earnest ones considered that such films as the "Three Musketeers" and "Monsieur Beaucaire" were quite sufficiently improving. So far they had had a little "Bring and Buy Sale" in aid of it, and had raised five and elevenpence three farthings, but as Mrs. Bruce Monkton-Bruce had said that was not nearly enough because they wanted a really good one.

The play was the suggestion of one of the new members, a Miss Gwladwyn. "That ought," she said optimistically, "to bring us in another pound or two."

The tradition of the Christmas Eve plays in the village included a silver collection at the door, but did not include tickets. It was rightly felt that if the village had to pay for its tickets, it would not come at all. The silver collection at the door, too, was not as lucrative as one would think because the village had no compunction at all about walking past the plate as if it did not see it even if it was held out right under its nose. It was felt generally that "a pound or two" was a rather too hopeful estimate. But still a pound, as Mrs. Bruce Monkton-Bruce so unanswerably pointed out, was a pound, and anyway it would be good for the Literary Society to get up a play. It would, she said, with her incurable optimism, "draw them together." As a matter of fact, experience had frequently proved the acting of a play to have precisely the opposite effect. . . . They held a meeting to discuss the nature of the play. There was an uneasy feeling that they ought to do one of Shakespeare's or Sheridan's, or, as Miss Formester put it, vaguely, "something of Shelley's or Keats'," but the more modest ones thought that though literary, they were not quite as literary as that, and the less modest ones, as represented by Mrs. Bruce Monkton-Bruce, said quite boldly and openly that though those authors had doubtless suited their own generations, things had progressed since then. She added that she'd once tried to read "She Stoops to Conquer," and hadn't been able to see what people saw in it.

"Of course," admitted Miss Georgine Hemmersley, "the men characters will be the difficulty." (The rembership of the Literary Society was entirely feminine.) "I have often thought that perhaps it would be a good thing to try to interest the men of the neighbourhood in our little society."

"I don't know," said Miss Featherstone doubtfully, thinking of those pleasant little meetings of the Literary Society, which were devoted to strong tea, iced cakes, and interchanges of local scandal. "I don't know. Look at it how you will as soon as you begin to have men in a thing, it complicates it at once. I've often noticed it. There's something *restless* about men. And they aren't literary. It's no good pretending they are."

The Society sighed and agreed.

"Of course it has its disavantages at a time like this," went on Miss Featherstone, "not having any men, I mean, because, of course, it means that we can't act any modern plays. It means we have to fall back on plays of historical times. I mean wigs and things."

"I know," said Miss Gwladwyn demurely, "a perfectly sweet little historical play."

"What period is it, dear?" said Mrs. Bruce Monkton-Bruce.

"It's the costume period," said Miss Gwladwyn simply. "You know. Wigs and ruffles and swords. Tudor. Or is it Elizabethan? It's about the Civil War, anyway, and it's really awfully sweet."

"What's the plot of it?" said the Literary Society with interest.

"Well," said Miss Gwladwyn, "the heroine" (a certain modest bashfulness in Miss Gwladwyn's mien at this moment showed clearly that she expected to be the heroine), "the heroine is engaged to a Roundhead, but she isn't really in love with him. At least she thinks she is, but she isn't. And a wounded Cavalier comes to her house to take refuge in a terrible storm, and she takes him in meaning to hand him over to her *fiancé*, you know. Her father's a Roundhead, of course, you see. And then she falls in love with him, with the Cavalier, I mean, and hides him, and then the *fiancé* finds him and she tells him that she doesn't love him, but she loves the other. That's an awfully sweet scene. There's a snow-storm. I've forgotten exactly how the snow-storm comes in, but I know that there is one, and it's awfully effective. You do it with tiny bits of paper dropped from above. It makes an awfully sweet scene. There are heaps of characters too," she went on eagerly, "we could *all* have quite good parts. There's a comic aunt and a comic uncle and awfully sweet parts for my—I mean her parents and quite a lot of servants with really *good* parts. There'd be parts and to spare for *everyone*. Some of us could even take two. It's an awfully sweet thing altogether."

Mrs. Bruce Monkton-Bruce looked doubtful.

"Is it *literary* enough, do you think," she said uncertainly.

"Oh *yes*," said Miss Gwladwyn, earnestly. "It *must* be. If it's historical it *must* be literary, mustn't it? I mean, it *follows*, doesn't it?"

Apparently the majority of the Literary Society thought it did.

"Anyway," said Miss Gwladwyn brightly, "I'll get the book and we'll have a reading and then vote on it. All I can say is that I've *seen* it and I've seen a good many of Shakespeare's plays too, and I consider this a much sweeter thing than any of Shakespeare's, and if that doesn't prove that it's Literary I don't know what does."

Again the Society seemed to find the logic unassailable and the meeting broke up (after tea and iced cake, a verbatim account of what Mrs. Jones said to Mrs. Robinson when they'd quarrelled last week, and a detailed description of the doctor's wife's new hat), arranging to meet the next week and read Miss Gwladwyn's play.

"I *know* that you'll like it," was Miss Gwladwyn's final assurance as she took her leave. "It's such an awfully sweet little thing."

* * *

The meeting took place early the next week. Miss Gwladwyn opened it by artlessly suggesting that as she'd seen the play before she should read the heroine's part.

It was generally felt that as she had introduced the play to them, this was only her due.

The first scene was read fairly briskly. It abounded, however, in such stage directions as "When door opens howling of wind is heard outside." "Crash of thunder without," and such remarks as: "Hark how the storm does rage to-night," and: "Hear the beating of the rain upon the window-panes." "Listen! Do you not hear the sound of horses' hoofs?"

At the end of the scene Miss Georgine Hemmerseley (who was a notorious pessimist) remarked:

"It will be very difficult to get those noises made."

"Those who aren't on the stage must make them," said Miss Gwladwyn.

"But we're all on the stage in this scene," objected Miss Georgine Hemmersley.

"Then we must have a special person to make them," said Miss Gwladwyn.

Miss Georgine Hemmersley threw her eye over the stage directions.

"They'll be very difficult to make," she said, "especially the wind. How does one make the sound of wind?"

"A sort of whistle, I suppose," said Miss Gwladwyn doubtfully.

"Y-yes," said Miss Georgine Hemmersley, "but *how?* I mean, *I* couldn't do it, for instance."

At that moment William passed down the street outside.

William was whistling—not his usual piercing blast of a whistle, but a slow, mournful, meditative whistle. As a matter of fact he was not aware that he was whistling at all. His mind was occupied with a deep and apparently insoluble problem—the problem of how to obtain a new football with no money or credit at his disposal. Only such an optimist as William would have tackled the problem at all. But William walking down the street, hands in pockets, scowling gaze fixed on the ground mechanically and unconsciously emitting a tuneless monotonous undertone of a whistle, was convinced that there must be a solution of the problem if only he could think of it. . . . If only he could think of it. . . . He passed by Mrs. Bruce Monkton-Bruce's open window and his whistle fell upon a sudden silence within.

"What's that?" said Mrs. Bruce Monkton-Bruce.

Miss Georgine Hemmersley went to the window.

"It's just a boy," she said.

Miss Gwladwyn followed her.

"It's that rough-looking boy one sees about so much," she said.

Mrs. Bruce Monkton-Bruce joined them at the window.

"It's William Brown," she said.

They stood at the open window while William, wholly unconscious of their regard, still grappling mentally with his insoluble problem, passed on his way. His faint tuneless strain floated back to them.

"It—it *does* sound like the wind," said Miss Gwladwyn.

On an impulse Mrs. Bruce Monkton-Bruce put her head out of the window.

"William Brown!" she called sharply. "Come here."

William turned and scowled at her aggressively.

"I've not done nothin'," he said. "It wasn't *me* you saw chasin' your cat yesterday."

"Come in here, William," she said. "We want to ask you something."

William stood hesitating, not sure whether to obey or whether to show his contempt of her by continuing his thoughtful progress down the street.

They probably only wanted him in to make a fuss about something he'd not done. Well, not *meant* to do anyway; well, not worth making a fuss about anyway. On the other hand it might be something else and if he went on he'd never know what they'd wanted him for. His curiosity won the day.

Taking a piece of chewing-gun, which he had absently been carrying in his mouth, from his mouth to his pocket, he proceeded to hoist himself up to the window-sill whence he had been summoned.

"*Not* that way, William!" said Mrs. Bruce Monkton-Bruce sternly. "Come in by the front door, please, in the usual way."

William lowered himself to the street again, put the chewing-gum back into his mouth, stood for a minute obviously wondering whether it was worth while to go in by the front door in the usual way, decided apparently that though it probably wasn't, still there was just a chance that it might be, then, very, very slowly (as if to prove his complete independence, despite his show of obedience), went round to the front door.

"You may open the door and come in," called Mrs. Bruce Monkton-Bruce from the window, "and don't forget to wipe your feet."

William opened the door and came in. He wiped his feet with a commendable and very lengthy thoroughness (whose object was to keep them waiting for him as long as possible), transferred his chewing-gum from his mouth to his pocket again, carefully arranged his cap between the horns of the stuffed head of an antelope which was hanging on the wall, thought better of it and transferred it to the stuffed head of a fox, which was hanging on the opposite wall, gazed critically for a long time at a stuffed owl in a cage, absently broke off a piece of a fern that grew in a plant pot next to the hat-stand,

"WILLIAM BROWN," MRS. MONKTON-BRUCE CALLED SHARPLY. "COME HERE!"

WILLIAM SCOWLED AGGRESSIVELY. "I'VE NOT DONE NOTHIN'," HE SAID.

and finally entered the drawing-room. He stood in the doorway facing them, still scowling aggressively and scattering bits of fern upon the carpet. His mind went quickly over the more recent events of his career in order to account for the summons. He was already regretting having obeyed it. He decided to take the offensive. Fixing a stern and scowling gaze upon Miss Greene-Joanes, he said:

"When you saw me in your garden yesterday I was jus' gettin' a ball of mine that'd gone over the wall into your garden. I was simply tryin' to save you trouble by goin' an' getting' it myself, 'stead of troublin' you goin' to the front door. An' that apple was one what I found lyin' under your tree an' I thought I'd pick it up for you jus' to help you tidy up the place 'cause it looks so untidy with apples lyin' about under the trees all over the place."

"William," said Mrs. Bruce Monkton-Bruce, "we did not ask you to come in in order to discuss your visit to Miss Greene-Joanes' garden——"

William turned his steely eyes upon her and pursued his policy of taking the offensive.

"Those stones you saw me throwin' at your tree," he said, "was jus' to kill grubs 'n' things what might be doin' it harm. I thought I'd help you keep your garden nice by throwin' stones at your tree to kill the grubs 'n' things on it for you 'cause they were eatin' away the bark or somethin'."

"We didn't bring you in to talk about that either, William," said Mrs. Bruce Monkton-Bruce. Then, clearing her throat, she said: "You were whistling as you went down the road, were you not?"

William's stern and freckled countenance expressed horror and amazement.

"*Well!*" he said. "*Well!* I bet I was hardly makin' any

noise at all. 'Sides"—aggressively— "there's nothin' to stop folks jus' *whistlin'*, is there? In the *street.* If they *want* to. I wasn't doin' you any *harm*, was I? Jus' *whistlin'* in the *street.* If you've gotta headache or anythin' an' don' want me to I won't not till I get into the nex' street where you won't hear me. Not now I know. You needn't've brought me *in* jus, to say that. If you'd jus' shouted it out of the window I'd 've heard all right. But I don't see you can blame me jus' for——"

Mrs. Bruce Monkton-Bruce held out a hand feebly to stem the tide of his eloquence.

"It's not that, William," she said faintly. "Do stop talking for two minutes, and let me speak. We—we were *interested* in your whistle. Would you—would you kindly repeat it in here—just to let us hear again what it sounds like?"

William was proud of his whistle and flattered to be thus asked to perform in public. He paused a minute to gather his forces together, drew in his breath, then emitted a sound that would have done credit to a factory syren.

Miss Georgine Hammersley screamed. Miss Gwladwyn, who was poised girlishly on the arm of her chair, lost her balance and fell on to the floor. Mrs. Bruce Monkton-Bruce clapped her hands to her ears with a moan of agony and Miss Greene-Joanes lay back in her chair in a dead faint, from which, however, as no one took any notice of her, she quickly recovered. William, immensely flattered by this reception of his performance, murmured modestly:

"I can do a better one still this way," and proceeded to put a finger into each corner of his mouth and to draw in his breath for another blast.

With great presence of mind, Mrs. Bruce Monkton-Bruce managed to put her hand across his face just in time.

"No, William," she said brokenly, "not like that—not like that——"

"I warn you," said Miss Greene-Joanes, in a shrill, trembling voice, "I shall have hysterics if he does it again. I've already fainted," she went on, in a reproachful voice, "but nobody noticed me. I won't be answerable for what happens to me if that boy stays in the room a minute longer."

"Send him away," moaned Miss Featherstone, "and let's *imagine* the wind."

"Let's leave it to chance," pleaded Miss Greene-Joanes. "I can't bear it again. There—there may be a *natural* wind that night. It's quite possible."

"William," said Mrs. Bruce Monkton-Bruce weakly, "it was a gentle whistle we wanted to hear. A whistle like—like—like the wind in the distance. A *long* way in the distance, William."

William emitted a gentle, drawn-out, mournful whistle. It represented perfectly the distant moaning of the wind. His stricken audience recovered and gave a gasp of amazement and delight.

"That was *very* nice," said Mrs. Bruce Monkton-Bruce.

William, cheered and flattered by her praise, said: "I'll do it a bit nearer than that now," and again gathered his forces for the effort.

"No, William," said Mrs. Bruce Monkton-Bruce again stopping him just in time. "That's as near as we want. That's *just* what we want. . . . Now, William, we are going to get up a little play, and during the play the wind is supposed to be heard right in the distance—a long, *long* way in the distance, William. The wind is supposed to be a *very* distant one indeed, William. Perhaps for a very great treat we'll let you make that wind, William."

William's mind worked quickly. The apparently insoluble problem was still with him. He saw a means, not to solve it indeed, but to make it a little less insoluble. Assuming his most sphinx-like expression he said unblushingly, unblinkingly:

"Well, of course—that'll take up a good deal of my time. I dunno *quite* as I can spare all that time."

They were amazed at his effrontery and at the same time his astounding and unexpected reluctance to accept the post of wind-maker increased the desirability of his whistle in their eyes.

"Of course, William," said Mrs. Bruce Monkton-Bruce in cold reproach, "if you don't want to help in a good cause like this——" Wisely she kept the exact nature of the good cause vague.

"Oh, I don' mind *helpin'*," said William; "all I meant was that it'd probably be takin' up a good deal of my time when I might be doin' useful things for other people. F'rinstance, I often pump up my uncle's motor tyres for him." William's face became so expressionless as to border on the imbecile as he added: "He always gives me sixpence for doing that."

There was a short silence and then Mrs. Bruce Monkton-Bruce said with great dignity:

"We will, of course, be pleased to give you sixpence for being the wind and any other little noises that may come into the play, William."

"Thank you," said William, concealing his delight beneath a tone of calm indifference. Sixpence . . . it was something to start from. William was such an optimist that with the first sixpence the whole fund seemed suddenly to be assured to him. . . . He could do something else for someone else and get another sixpence and that would be a shilling, and, well, if he kept on doing things for people for sixpence he'd soon have enough money to buy the football. Optimistically he ignored the fact that most people expected him to do things for them for nothing. . . .

It was arranged that William should attend the next reading of the play in order to be the wind and whatever other noises might be necessary and then William, transferring his chewing-gum from his pocket to his mouth and scattering bits of fern absently to mark his path as he went, disappeared into the hall, took his cap from the fox's head, pulled a face at the stuffed owl, then, seeming annoyed by its equanimity, pulled another, absently plucked off another spray of Mrs. Bruce Monkton-Bruce's cherished fern, and made his devastating way into the street. His piercing and unharmonious whistle shattered the quiet of countless peaceful homes as he strode onwards, cheered and invigorated by his visit, looking forward with equal joy to his rôle as wind-maker and his possession of the sixpence that was to be the nucleus of his football fund.

The members of the Literary Society heaved sighs of relief as the sounds of his departure faded into the distance.

"Don't you think," said Miss Greene-Joanes pathetically, "that we could find a *quieter* type of boy."

"But it *was*," said Mrs. Bruce Monkton-Bruce, "it *was* a *very* good imitation of the wind. I mean, of course, when he did it softly."

"But wouldn't a quieter type of boy do?" persisted Miss Greene-Joanes. "For instance, there's that dear little Cuthbert Montgomery."

"But he can't whistle," objected Mrs. Bruce Monkton-Bruce. "I'm afraid that you'd always find that the quiet type of boy couldn't do such a good whistle."

So reluctantly the Literary Society decided to appoint William as the wind.

* * *

William put in an early appearance at the next rehearsal. It was in fact a little too early for Mrs. Bruce Monkton-Bruce, at whose house it was held. He arrived half an hour before the time at which it was to begin and spent the half-hour sitting in her drawing-room cracking nuts and practising his whistle. Mrs. Bruce Monkton-Bruce said that it gave her a headache that lasted for a week.

"William," she said sternly when she entered the drawing-room, "if you don't learn to do a *quiet* whistle we won't have you at all."

"*Wasn't* that quiet?" said William, surprised. "It seemed to me to be such a quiet sort of whistle that I'm surprised you heard it at all."

"Well, I *did*," she snapped, "and it's given me a headache, and don't do it any more."

"Sorry," said William succinctly, transferring his whole attention to his nuts.

Her tone had conveyed to him that his position as wind-maker was rather precarious, so when the other members of the cast arrived he made his wind whistle so low that they had to request him to do it a *leetle*—just a *very leetle*—louder. Even then it sounded very faint and far away. William had decided not to risk either his sixpence or his place in the cast by whistling too loudly at rehearsals. The actual performance of course would be quite a different matter. His gentle whistle endeared him to them. They unbent to him. He was turning out, Miss Featherstone confided to Miss Gwladwyn in a whisper, a nicer type of boy than she had feared he would at first. He had helpful suggestions too about the other noises. He knew how to make the sound of horses' hooves. You did it with a coco-nut. And he knew how to make thunder. You did it with a tin tray. And he could make revolver shots by letting off caps or squibs or something. Anyway, he could do it somehow. . . . They thought that perhaps he'd better not try those things till nearer the time. He'd better confine himself to the wind—so he confined himself to the wind, a gentle, anæmic sort of wind which he despised in his heart, but which he felt was winning him the confidence of his new friends. They unbent to him more and more. He was rather annoyed that he was not to have the snow-storm. Miss Gwladwyn said that her nephew would manage the snow-storm. She said that her nephew was a dear little boy with beautiful manners, who she admitted regretfully could not whistle, and might not be able to manage the other noises, but would, she was sure, manage the snow-storm perfectly.

William went home fortified by their praise of his distant whistle and two buns given him by Mrs. Bruce Monkton-Bruce. On the way he met Douglas and Henry and Ginger.

"Hello," they said, "where've you been?"

"I've been to a rehearsal," said William with his own inimitable swagger. "I'm actin' in a play."

They were as impressed as even William could wish them to be.

"What play?" demanded Ginger.

"One the Lit'ry Society's gettin' up," said William airily.

"What's it called?" said Douglas.

William did not know what it was called, so he said with an air of careless importance:

"That's a secret. I've not got to tell anyone that."

"Well, what are you actin' in it?" said Henry.

William's swagger increased.

"I'm the most important person in it," he said. "They

jolly well couldn't do it at all without me."

"You the *hero?*" said Ginger incredulously.

"Um," admitted William. "That's what I am."

After all, he thought, surely in a play where you were continually hearing and talking about the wind, the wind might be referred to as the hero. Anyway, he soothed his conscience by telling it that as he was the only man in the piece, he *must* be the hero.

"They'll all women," he continued carefully, "so of course they had to get a man in from somewhere to be the hero."

The Outlaws were not quite convinced, and yet there was *something* about William's swagger. . . .

"Well," said Ginger, "I s'pose if you're the hero you'll be havin' rehearsals with 'em?"

"Yes," said William. "Course *I* will!"

"All right," challenged Ginger. "Tell us where you're havin' the nex' one an' we'll *see.*"

"At Mrs. Bruce's nex' Tuesday afternoon at three," said William promptly.

"All *right,*" said the Outlaws, "an' we'll jolly well *see.*"

So next Tuesday at three o'clock they jolly well *saw.* Hidden in the bushes in Mrs. Bruce Monkton-Bruce's (let us call her by her full name. She hated to hear it as she said "murdered") garden they saw the cast of "A Trial of Love" arrive one by one at the front door. And with them arrived William—the only male character—swaggering self-consciously but quite obviously as an invited guest up Mrs. Bruce Monkton-Bruce's front drive. He was fully aware of the presence of his friends in the bushes, though he appeared not to notice them. His swagger as he walked in at the front door is indescribable.

The Outlaws crept away silent and deeply impressed.

It was true. William must be the hero of the play. They were torn between envy of their leader and pride in him. Though all of them would have liked to be the hero of a play, still they could shine in William's reflected glory. Their walk as they went away from Mrs. Bruce Monkton-Bruce's front gate reflected something of William's swagger. William was a hero in a play. Well, people'd have to treat them *all* a bit diff'rent after that.

The rehearsal was on the whole a great success. William, afraid that his friends might be listening at the window and not wishing them to guess the comparative insignificance of his rôle, reduced his whistle to a mere breath. Mrs. Bruce Monkton-Bruce said encouragingly: "Just a *leetle* louder, William," but Miss Greene-Jones said hastily: "Well, perhaps it would be as well to keep it like that for rehearsals, dear, and to bring it out just a *leetle* bit louder on the night."

So William, still afraid that the Outlaws were crouched intently outside the window, kept it like that.

It was decided at the end that William need not attend all the rehearsals. The cast found his stare demoralising, and his habit of transferring his piece of chewing-gum (he'd had it for three weeks now) from his mouth to his pocket and from his pocket to his mouth disconcerting. Also he would at intervals take a nut from another pocket and crack it with much noise and facial contortion. He always made a very ostentatious show of collecting all the shells and putting them into yet another pocket, but Mrs. Bruce Monkton-Bruce's horrified gaze watched a little heap of broken nutshells steadily growing upon her precious carpet by William's feet. William himself fondly imagined that he was behaving in an exemplary way. He had even offered each of them one of his nuts and had been secretly much relieved at their refusal. They could not, he thought, expect him to offer them a chew of his chewing-gum. . . . But he was supremely bored and was not sorry when informed that it would be best for them to rehearse the play without wind and thunder till they were a little more accustomed to it.

He was not summoned to another rehearsal for a fortnight. The play was, as Miss Georgina Hemmersley said "taking shape beautifully." Miss Georgina Hemmersley as a Cavalier looked quite dashing, despite her forty-odd years, and Miss Featherstone as the Roundhead looked also very fine, though she too had passed her first youth. It was, however, as she said, only fair that those who had been in the society longest should have the best parts. . . . Miss Gwladwyn, they all agreed, made a sweetly pretty heroine.

William arrived with all his paraphernalia of coco-nuts and squibs and tin tray, and, he considered, put up the best show of all of them. True, the rest of the cast seemed a little irritable. They kept saying: "*Quietly*, William." "William, not so *loud*." "William, we can't hear ourselves speak." "William, stop making that *deafening* noise. Well, there isn't any wind now." At the end Miss Greene-Joanes, who had seemed strangely excited all the time, burst out:

"Now, I've got some news for you all. . . . William, you needn't stay." William began to make elaborate and protracted preparations for his departure, but, intensely curious, lingered within earshot. "I didn't tell you before we began, because I knew it would make you too excited to act. It did me. You'll never *guess* who's staying in the village."

"*Who?*" chorused the cast breathlessly.

"Sir Giles Hampton."

The cast uttered screams of excitement. The Cavalier said, "What for?" and the Roundhead said, "Who told you?" and the comic aunt and uncle said simultaneously, "Good *heavens!*"

"He's had a nervous breakdown," said Miss Greene-Joanes, "and he's staying at the inn here because of the air, and he's supposed to be incognito, but of *course* people recognise him. As a matter of fact, he's telling people who he is because he's not *really* keen on being incognito. Actors never are really. They feel frightfully mad if people don't recognise them."

"What's he like to look at?" said the comic aunt breathlessly.

"Tall and important-looking and rather handsome with very bushy eyebrows."

"Do you think he'll *come?*" said all the cast simultaneously.

"I don't know but—— William, *will* you go home and stop dropping nutshells on the carpet."

There was a silence while all the cast waited impatiently for William to take his leave. With great dignity William took it. He was annoyed at his unceremonious ejection. Thinking such a lot of themselves and their old play, and where would they be, he'd like to know, without the wind and the thunder and the horses' hooves and all the rest of it? . . . Treating the most important person in the play the way they treated him. . . .

He walked down the road scowling morosely, absent-mindedly cracking nuts and scattering nut-shells about him as he went. . . . At the end of the road he collided with a tall man with bushy eyebrows.

"You should look where you're going, my little man," said the stranger.

"Come to that, so should you," remarked William, who was still feeling embittered.

The tall man blinked.

"Do you know who I am?" he said majestically.

"No," said William simply, "an' I bet you don't know who I am either."

"I am a very great actor," said the man.

"So'm I," said William promptly.

"So great," went on the man, "that when they want me to play a part they give me any money I choose to ask for it."

"I'm that sort, too," said William, thrusting his hands deep into his trouble pockets. "I asked for sixpence an' they gave it me straight off. It's goin' to a new football."

"And do you know why I'm here, my little man?" said the stranger.

"No," said William without much interest and added: "I'm here because I live here."

"I'm here," said the man, "because of my nerves. Acting has exhausted my vitality and impaired my nervous system. I'm an artist, and like most other artists am highly strung. Do you know that sometimes before I go on to the stage I tremble from head to foot."

"I don't," said William coolly. "I never feel like that when I'm actin'."

"Ah!" smiled the man, "but I'm always the most important person in the plays I act in."

"S'm I," retorted William. "I'm like that. I'm the most important person in the play I'm in now."

"Would you like to see the programme of the play I've just been acting in in London?" continued the actor, taking a piece of paper out of his pocket.

William looked at it with interest. It contained a list of names in ordinary-sized print; then an "and" and then "Giles Hampton" in large letters.

"Yes," said William calmly, "that's the way my name's going' to be printed in our play."

"What play is it?" said the man yielding at last to

William's irresistible egotism.

"It's called 'The Trial of Love,'' said William. "It's for my football an' their cinematograph."

"Ha-ha!" said the man. "And may—may—ah—distinguished strangers come to it?"

"Yes," said William casually, "*anyone* can come to it. You've gotter pay at least. Everyone's gotter pay."

"Well, I must certainly come," said the distinguished stranger. "I must certainly come and see you play the hero."

* * *

The dress rehearsal was not an unqualified success, but as Miss Featherstone said that was always a sign that the real performance would go off well. In all the most successful plays, she said, the dress rehearsal went off badly. William quite dispassionately considered them the worst-tempered set of people he'd ever come across in his life. They snapped at him if he so much as spoke. They said that his wind was far too loud, though it was in his opinion so faint and distant a breeze that it was hardly worth doing at all. They objected also to his thunder and his horses' hooves. They said quite untruly that they were deafening. A deep disgust with the whole proceedings was growing stronger and stronger in William's breast. He felt that it would serve them right if he washed his hands of the whole thing and refused to make any of their noises for them. The only reason why he did not do this was that he was afraid that if he did they'd find some one else to do it in his place. Moreover he was feeling worried about another matter. He was aware that he did not take in the play such an important part as he had given his friends to understand. He had given them to understand that he took the principal part and was on the stage all the time, whereas, though he quite honestly considered that he took the principal part, he wasn't on the stage at all. Then there was that man with bushy eye-brows he'd met in the village. He'd probably come, and William had quite given him to understand that he had his name on the programme in big letters and took a principal part. . . .

"*Thunder*, William," said Miss Gwladwyn irritably, interrupting his meditations. "Why don't you keep awake and follow where we are!"

William emitted a piercing whistle.

"Not *wind*," she snapped. "*Thunder*."

William beat on his tin tray.

Miss Greene-Joanes groaned.

"That noise," she said, "goes through and *through* my head. I can't bear it!"

"Well, thunder is loud," said William coldly. "It's nachrally loud. I can't help thunder being' nachrally loud."

"Thunder more gently, William," commanded Mrs. Bruce Monkton-Bruce.

Just to annoy them William made an almost inaudible rumble of thunder, but to his own great annoyance it didn't annoy them at all. "That's better, William," they said; and gloomily William returned to his meditation. He'd seen the programme and had hardly been able to believe his eyes when he saw that his name wasn't on it at all. They hadn't even got his name down as the wind or the thunder or the horses' hooves or anything. . . . If it hadn't been for that sixpence he'd certainly have chucked up the whole thing. . . .

They'd got to the snow-storm scene now. The curtains were half drawn across and in the narrow aperture appeared Miss Gwladwyn, the heroine. It was a very complicated plot, but at this stage of it she'd been turned out of her home by her cruel Roundhead father and was wandering in search of her lost Cavalier lover.

She said: "How cold it is! Heaven, wilt thou show me any pity?" and turned her face up to the sky, and tiny snow-flakes began to fall upon her face. The tiny snow-flakes were tiny bits of paper dropped down through a tiny opening in the ceiling by her well-mannered little nephew. He did it very nicely. William did not pay much attention to it. He was beginning to consider the whole thing beneath his contempt.

* * *

It was the evening of the performance. The performers were making frenzied preparations behind the scenes. Mr. Fleuster was to draw the curtain, Miss Featherstone's sister was to prompt, and William was to hand out programmes. Mr. Fleuster has not come into this story before, but he had been trying to propose to Miss Gwladwyn for the last five years and had not yet been able to manage it. Both Miss Gwladwyn and Miss Gwladwyn's friends had given him ample opportunities, but opportunities only seemed to make him yet more bashful. When he had not an opportunity he longed to propose, and when an opportunity of proposing came he lost his head and didn't do it. Miss Gwladwyn had done everything a really nice woman can do; that is to say, she had done everything short of actually proposing herself. Her friends had arranged for him to draw the curtain in the hopes that it would bring matters to a head. Not that they really expected that it would. It would, of course, be a good opportunity, and as such would fill him with terror and dismay.

Mr. Fleuster, large and perspiring, stood by the curtain, pretending not to see that Miss Gwladwyn was standing quite near him and that no one else was within earshot, and that it was an excellent opportunity.

William stood sphinx-like at the door distributing programmes. His cogitations had not been entirely profitless. He had devised means by which he hoped to vindicate his position as hero. For one thing he had laboriously printed out four special programmes which he held concealed beneath the ordinary programmes, and which were to be distributed to Ginger, Douglas, Henry, and the actor, if the actor should come. He had copied down the dramatis personæ from the ordinary programme, but at the end he had put an "and" and then in gigantic letters:

Wind	Shots	} William Brown.
Rain	And All	
Thunder	Other Noises	
Horses' Hooves		

Seeing Ginger coming he hastily got one of his home-made programmes out and assuming his blankest expression handed it to him.

"Good ole William," murmured Ginger as he took it.

Then Henry came, and Henry also was given one.

"Why aren't you changin' into your things?" said Henry.

"I don't *ackshully* come on to the stage," admitted William. "I'm the most important person in the play as you'll soon jolly well see, but I don't *ackshully* come on to the stage."

He was glad to have got that confession off his chest.

Then Douglas came. He handed the third of his privately printed programmes to Douglas with an air of impersonal offialism, as if he were too deeply occupied in his duties to be able to recognise his friends.

There was only one left. That was for the actor. If the actor came. William peered anxiously down the road.

The room was full. It was time to begin.

"William Brown!" an exasperated voice hissed down the room. William swelled with importance. Everyone would know now that they couldn't begin without him. He continued to gaze anxiously down the road. There he was at last.

"William *Brown!*"

The actor was almost at the door. He carried a parcel under his arm.

"William Brown," said someone in the back row obligingly, "they want you."

"*William—Brown!*" hissed Mrs. Bruce Monkton-Bruce's face, appearing frenzied and bodiless like the Cheshire cat between the curtains.

The actor entered the hall. William thrust his one remaining programme into his hand.

"Thought you were the hero," said the actor, gazing at him sardonically.

William met his sardonic gaze unblinkingly.

"So I am," he said promptly, "but the hero doesn't *always* come on to the stage. Not in the *newest* sort of plays, anyway." He pointed to the large-lettered part of the programme. "That's me," he said modestly. "All of it's me."

With this he hastened back behind the curtain, leaving the actor reading his programme at the end of the room.

He was received with acrimony by a nerve-racked cast.

"Keeping us all waiting all this time."

"Didn't you *hear* us calling?"

"It's nearly twenty-five to."

"It's all right," said William in a superior manner that maddened them still further. "You can begin now."

Miss Featherstone's sister took her prompt-book, Mr. Fleuster seized the curtain-strings, the cast entered the stage, William took his seat behind, and the play began.

Now William's plans for making himself the central figure of the play did not stop with the programmes. He considered that the noises he had been allowed to make at the rehearsals had been pitifully inadequate, and he intended to-night to produce a storm more worthy of his powers. Who ever heard of the wind howling in a storm the way they'd made him howl all these weeks? He knew what the wind howling in a storm sounded like and he'd jolly well make it sound like that. There was his cue. Someone was saying:

"Hark how the storm rages. Canst hear the wind?"

At the ensuing sound the prompter dropped her book and the heroine lost her balance and brought down the property mantelpiece on to the top of her. William had put a finger into each corner of his mouth in order to aid nature in the rendering of the storm. The sound was even more piercing than he had expected it to be. *That*, thought William, complacently noticing the havoc it played with both audience and cast, was something like a wind. That would show 'em whether he was the hero of the play or not. With admirable presence of mind the cast pulled itself together and continued. William's next cue was the thunder.

"List," said the heroine, "how the thunder rages in the valley."

The thunder raged and continued to rage. For some minutes the cast remained silent and motionless—except for facial contortions expressive of horror and despair—waiting for the thunder to abate, but as it showed no signs of stopping they tried to proceed. It was, however, raging so violently that no one could hear a word, so they had to stop again.

At last even its maker tired of it and it died away. The play proceeded. Behind the scenes William smiled again to himself. *That* had been a jolly good bit of thunder. He'd really enjoyed that. And it would jolly well let them all know he was there even if he wasn't dressed up and on the stage like the others. His next cue was the horses' hooves, and William was feeling a little nervous about that. The sound of horses' hooves is made with a coco-nut, and though William had managed to take his coco-nut (purchased for him by Mrs. Bruce Monkton-Bruce) about with him all the time the play was in rehearsal, he had as recently as last night succumbed to temptation and eaten it. He didn't quite know what to do about the horses' hooves. He hadn't dared to tell anyone about it. But still he thought he'd be able to manage it. Here it was coming now.

"Listen," Miss Gwladwyn was saying. "I hear the sound of horses' hooves."

Then in the silence came the sound of a tin tray being hit slowly, loudly, regularly. The audience gave a yell of laughter. William felt annoyed. He hadn't meant it to sound like that. It wasn't anything to laugh at, anyway. He showed his annoyance by another deafening and protracted thunderstorm.

When this had died away the play proceeded. William's part in that scene was officially over. But William did not wish to withdraw from the public eye. It occurred to him that in all probability the wind and the thunder still continued. Yes, somebody mentioned again that it was a wild night to be out in. Come to that, the war must be going on all the time. There were probably battles going on all over the place. He'd better throw a few squibs about and make a bit more wind and thunder. He set to work with commendable thoroughness.

At last the end of the scene came. Mr. Fleuster drew the curtains and chaos reigned. Most of the cast attacked William, but some of them were attacking each other, and quite a lot of them were attacking the prompter. They had on several occasions forgotten their words and not once had the prompter come to their rescue. On one occasion they had wandered on to Act II and stayed there a considerable time. The prompter's plea that she'd lost her place right at the very beginning and hadn't been able to find it again was not accepted as an excuse. Then Miss Hemmersley was annoyed with Miss Featherstone for giving her the wrong cues all the way through, and Miss Gwladwyn was annoyed with Miss Greene-Joanes for cutting into her monologue, and Miss Greene-Joanes was annoyed with Mrs. Bruce Monkton-Bruce for standing just where she prevented the audience having a good view of her (Miss Greene-Joanes), and when they couldn't find anyone else to be annoyed with they turned on William. Fortunately for William, however, there was little time for recrimination, as already the audience was clamouring for the second scene. This was the snow-storm scene. Miss Gwladwyn had installed her beautifully-mannered nephew in the loft early in the evening with a box of chocolate creams to keep him quiet. Miss Gwladwyn went on to the stage. The other actors retired to the improvised green-room, there to continue their acrimonious disputes and mutual reproaches. The curtain was slightly drawn. Miss Gwladwyn went into the aperture and leapt into her pathetic monologue, and William behind the scenes relapsed into boredom. He was roused from by Miss Gwladwyn's nephew who came down the steps of the loft carrying an empty chocolate box and looking green.

"William," he said, "will you do my thing for me? I'm going to be sick."

"All right," said William distantly. "What do you do?"

William, not having been chosen as the snow-storm, had never taken the slightest interest in the snow-storm scene.

"You just get the bucket in the corridor and take it up to the loft and empty it over her slowly when she turns up her face."

"A' right," said William with an air of graciousness, secretly not sorry to add the snow-storm to his repertoire. "A' right. I'll carry on. Don' you worry. You go home an' be sick."

It was not William's fault that someone had put the stage fireplace in the passage in such a position that it completely hid the bucket of torn-up paper and that the only bucket visible in the passage was the bucket of water thoughtfully placed there by Mrs. Bruce Monkton-Bruce in case of fire. William looked about him, saw what was apparently the only bucket in the passage, took it up and went to the stairs leading into the loft. It was jolly heavy. Water! Crumbs! He hadn't realised it was water. He'd had an idea that it was torn-up paper for snow, but probably they'd changed their minds at the last minute and thought they'd have rain instead. Or perhaps they'd only had paper for the rehearsals, and had meant to have water for the real performance all along. Well, certainly it *was* a bit more exciting than paper. He took it very carefully up the stairs, then knelt over the little opening where he could see Miss Gwladwyn down below. He was only just in time. She was already saying:

"How cold it is! Heaven, wilt thou show me no pity?"

Then slowly and with a beautiful gesture of despair she raised her face towards the ceiling to receive full and square the entire contents of a bucket of water. William tried conscientiously to do it slowly, but it was a heavy bucket and he had to empty it all at once. He considered

SLOWLY, WITH A BEAUTIFUL GESTURE OF DESPAIR, MISS GWLADWYN LOOKED UPWARD AT THE CEILING—TO RECEIVE, FULL AND SQUARE IN HER FACE, THE CONTENTS OF WILLIAM'S BUCKET OF WATER.

that he was rather clever in hitting her face so exactly. For a moment the audience enjoyed the spectacle of Miss Gwladwyn sitting on the floor, dripping wet and gasping and spluttering. Then Mr. Fleuster had the presence of mind to draw the curtain. After which he deliberately walked across to the dripping, spluttering, gasping Miss Gwladwyn and asked her to marry him. For five years he'd been trying to propose to a dignified and very correctly dressed and mannered Miss Gwladwyn, and he'd never had the courage, but as soon as he saw her gasping, spluttering, dripping on the floor like that he knew that now was the moment or never. And Miss Gwladwyn, still gasping, spluttering, dripping, said, "Yes."

Then the entire cast began to look for William. Somehow it never occurred to them to blame Miss Gwladwyn's guileless nephew. They knew by instinct who was responsible for the calamity. William, realising also by instinct that he had made a mistake, slipped out into the darkness.

He was stopped by a tall form that blocked his way.

"Ha!" said the tall man. "Going already? I realised, of course, the last scene must be the *grande finale*. I had meant to present this to you at the end, but pray accept it now."

He went away chuckling, and William found himself clasping the most magnificent football he had ever seen in his life.

And that was not all.

For the next day there arrived a magnificent cinematograph for the Literary Society, sent by Sir Giles Hampton with a little note telling them that their little play had completely cured his nervous breakdown, that it would be a precious memory to him all the rest of his life, and that he was going back to London cheered and invigorated.

And that was not all.

There arrived for William some weeks later a ticket for a box at a London theatre.

William went, accompanied by his mother.

He came back and told his friends about it.

He said he'd seen a play called *Macbeth*, but he didn't think much of it, and he could have made a better storm himself.

Chapter 3

William and the Archers

William and Ginger and Douglas (Henry was staying with an aunt) were engaged on their usual Monday morning pastime. A stream ran through the centre of the village, and flowed under the road at a point where the village worthies used to collect on fine Sunday afternoons and evenings to discuss local affairs, or to stand leaning against the railings gazing silently in front of them, deep, presumably, in thought, till bed-time. This little space by the railings was on Monday morning thickly covered with the matches with which the village worthies had lit their pipes or cigarettes. Ginger and William and Douglas carefully collected the matches. Then Ginger stood at one side of the road and put the matches into the stream, where it entered the large pipe which guided it beneath the road, and William stood at the other side with a little heap of stones and tried to hit the matches as they came out. Douglas stood by and acted as umpire. "Got it!" "Missed it!" he sang out blithely at intervals. Occasionally the game was held up by a dispute between William and Douglas as to whether some particular throw had been a hit or a miss. After a short time William changed rôles with Ginger, and Ginger tried to hit the matches as they came out. Spirited recrimination, insult and counter-insult, were hurled over the road.

"Fancy not hittin' *that* one!" said William. "Well, I c'n hardly *believe* you din't hit *that* one. It's the biggest match I've ever seen in all my life. I don't see how you could *help* hittin' that one. Almost as big as a rollin' pin."

"*Well!*" said Ginger. "Well, I like that. I've hit *hundreds* more'n you hit. *Thousands.* An' that—why, it was the *teeniest, teeniest* match I've ever seen. Not much bigger'n a pin."

"Well, jus' fancy not hittin' that great big, enormous match. Butter-fingers!"

They met joyfully in the middle of the road and were only separated by a motor car, which took the corner at a terrific speed and narrowly missed putting an end to all further exploits of the Outlaws. They picked themselves up from the road, their original quarrel forgotten in a joint fury against the driver of the car.

"Serve him right if he'd killed us," said Ginger, "an' got hung for it."

"No," said William. "I bet it'd be more fun for him not to get hung—but for us to haunt him. I bet if he'd killed us an' we'd turned into ghosts, we could have had awful fun haunting him—— I say"—warming to his theme—"I bet it would be as much fun as *anythin'* we've ever done, hauntin' someone, groanin' an' rattlin' chains an' scarin' 'em an' jumpin' out at 'em an' such like."

"Wouldn't he be *mad?*" chuckled Ginger, "an' he cun't *do* anything to us 'cause you can't to a ghost. When you hit 'em, the hit sort of goes through 'em, an' if they run after you, an' catch you, the catch sort of goes through you, an' anyway they're all scared stiff of jus' *lookin'* at you. Won't it be *fun* to have everyone scared stiff of jus' *lookin'* at you. I can think," he went on meditatively, "of quite a lot of people I'd like to haunt when I'm dead—Ole Markie an' Farmer Jenks an' people like that. I bet it'd be more *fun* bein' a ghost than *anythin'*—even a pirate."

"I dunno," said Douglas, "they can't *eat.* Jus' *think* of not bein' able to eat. Jus' *think* of seein' sweet shop windows full of sweets an' being able to get through doors an' things so's you could go into sweet shops at night when there was no one there lookin' after 'em and yet not be able to *eat.*"

"Are you sure you can't eat," said Ginger anxiously.

"Yes," said Douglas with great solemnity, "I *know* you can't. You put out your hand to take up a sweet an' your hand sort of keeps goin' through 'em and can't pick 'em up."

The Outlaws shuddered at this horrible prospect.

"If you're a pirate or a robber chief or even a Red Injun," went on Douglas, "it's jus' as excitin' an' you *can* eat."

The Outlaws agreed that on the whole it would be better to be pirates or robber chiefs or Red Indians than ghosts and returned to the pastime in which the passage of the motor car had disturbed them.

"Now go on," William admonished Ginger, "see if you c'n hit a match what's almost as big as—a—as a—as a—telegraph pole," he said with a burst of inspiration; "see if——"

Douglas interrupted.

"I'm gettin' a bit sick of umpirin'," he said.

"All right," said William generously. "All right. You can change places with Ginger an' Ginger umpire for a bit an' you hit—I bet you c'n hit better'n *him.*"

Ginger showed proper spirit in resenting this insult till the passage of another motor—at a more leisurely pace—again separated them. The driver leant over his seat, cursed them soundly and shook his fist at them. The

Outlaws sitting in the dust by the roadside whither they had rolled on the approach of the car sat and gazed after it in horror and indignation. William found his voice first.

"*Well!*" he said. "Well! *fancy* nearly *killin'* folks an' then talkin' like that to 'em. Coo—I'd like to haunt *him*."

"Oh, come on," said Douglas. "Gimme the stones and start puttin' the matches in an' I bet I hit every one."

But it was suddenly discovered that there were only two matches left and that Ginger and William were tired of the game. Despite Douglas' passionate protests they walked away from the stream, Douglas remarking bitterly:

"That's always the way. Always. *Always* with *everythin'!* The minute my turn for anythin' comes it stops."

"What shall we do?" said Ginger when they had walked aimlessly to the end of the road.

"Let's get out the bows and arrers an' practise," said William. "We've not done that for quite a long time."

So they got out their bows and arrows, fixed up a target on a tree in William's back garden and for some time practised happily enough. Only Douglas was still gloomy.

"Always the way," he muttered bitterly as he listlessly strung his bow. "Umpire for hours an' hours an' *hours* an' when my time comes only two matches left."

"You can have first go hittin' next Monday," said William generously.

"Yes," said Douglas, still bitter, "an' it'll be wet Sunday night an' they'll all stay indoors an' there won't be any matches. Oh, I *know!*"

He was further annoyed by the fact that he failed to score a bull.

"Always the same!" he said, "somethin' wrong with my arrers now. 'S'enough for me to get hold of a thing for everything to go wrong—an' anyway it's a silly sort of thing to do—shootin' with bows and arrers. Bow and arrer shootin' isn't any use to anyone but Normans an' Red Indians an' such like."

William who had scored several bulls spiritedly opposed this view.

"I bet it is," he said. "I bet it's more use than any other sort of shootin'!"

Douglas gave vent to his general sense of bitterness and disappointment by a derisive laugh. "Huh!" he said, "*Huh!* D'you mean to say that bow an' arrer shootin's more use than *gun* shootin' an' *pistol* shootin'? What about the war? Was there any bow an' arrer shootin' in the war? No. They only did gun shootin' an' pistol shootin' 'cause those is the only kinds of shootin' what's any good. D'you think that they'd have had only gun shootin' if bow an' arrer shootin' was any good?"

William, having taken up any position, was seldom at a loss in defending it.

"Huh!" he said repeating Douglas' derisive laugh, "*Huh!* Well, jus' at first gun shootin's better, of course. *Anyone* knows that. Jus' at *first*. Because they shoot with gunpowder and nat'rally gunpowder shoots *further* than string. Yes, but you listen . . . what about when all the gunpowder's used up? What about a war what goes on so long that all the gun-powder's used up? What'll they do *then?* They'll *have* to start shootin' with bows an' arrers *then*. Yes, an' they'll be in a nice mess too 'cause none of 'em'll know how to shoot 'em an' it's not as easy as it looks. Yes, they'll be jolly glad of *us* to teach 'em *then*. It's jolly lucky for them *we* know how to do it. I bet we'll all be made generals an' commander-in-chiefs then. I bet if there's another war they'll soon use up all the gunpowder 'cause with all the lot they used up in the last war there can't be much left an' *then we'll* come in with our bows an' arrers."

"Well, there's not many of us to fight against a whole foreign army," said Douglas gloomily. "Jus' you an' me an' Ginger an' Henry against a whole foreign army."

"Y-yes," admitted William reluctantly. Then he brightened. "But we could *train* some more. We could start trainin' 'em now so as to be ready."

It was not in William's nature, however, to spend much time preparing for remote contingencies. He added hastily, "'S not as if we'd have to wait till we were were grown up. I think that we ought to have a bow an' arrer army all ready an' it doesn't matter not bein' grown up for bows an' arrers. You can shoot 'em jus' as hard not grown up. Look at me," he swaggered, "two bulls' eyes straight after each other. Well, wot I think is this, that we oughter start right away makin' a bow an' arrer army. Wot I think is"—William was unconsciously lapsing into his platform manner—"that people aren't as careful as what they ought to be about foreign armies landin'. There's nothin' to stop 'em. They can jus' get into a ship an' sail over to England an' land same as anyone else an' here'll they be right in the middle of us before we know anythin' about it. Wot I say is that we oughter *do* somethin' now 'stead of waitin' an' waitin' an' *waitin'* till it's too late. Wot I say is that we might wake up to-morrow an' find the fields here full of foreign enemies what have sailed over in the night an' think what a long time it'd take to get our soldiers together an' to get gunpowder for their guns. Before they'd have time to do that the foreign enemy'd have conquered 'em. Well, wot I say is that if *we're* here with an army of bow and arrer shooters it'll be all right. Bows an' arrers don't need a lot of gettin' ready like guns—— If they break you can easy make another, an' we can go on usin' 'em long after they've used up all their gunpowder an' got nothin' left to shoot with. Well, wot I say is"—William, worked up for an oratorial climax, sought about in his mind for some striking and original remark and finding none repeated—"Wot I say is we've gotta get a bow an' arrer army."

Ginger and Douglas, carried away by this flow of eloquence, cheered loudly.

William collected his "bow an' arrer army" with surprising speed. The holidays were drawing to a close and most of his school friends and acquaintances were growing tired of their own resources and were willing to follow William wherever he led them. Some of them already possessed bows and arrows. Others bought them. Others made them. William assembled them on the first day on which they were fully equipped and harangued them.

"Soldiers," he said, "we've all gotter learn bow and arrer shootin' so as to be ready for when all the gunpowder in the world gets finished up which, of course, it must do sometime, same as coal, we've gotter be ready for when a foreign enemy comes suddenly over in ships by night an' is here right in the middle of England before anyone finds out. They'd be disguised, of course, till they started fightin'. Well, we've gotter be ready with our bows and arrers to fight 'em an' hold 'em at bay till the real army's got together an' got its guns an' gunpowder an' things, an' then we've gotter be ready to fight 'em again when all the gunpowder's used up. That's what we've gotter do, we've gotter be *ready*," William as ever was at this point fired by his own eloquence, "we've gotter be ready to save our country from the enemy, same as people like Moses an' Napoleon did. . . ."

"Napoleon din't," said a small child in the rear.

"Moses din't either," said another.

"Oh, they din't, din't they?" said William threateningly, annoyed at the interruption.

They looked at William. William after all was more real than Moses and Napoleon. It didn't matter what Moses and Napoleon had done. It did matter what William might do.

"All right then," they agreed pacifically, "they did then."

"Course they did," said William, "an' that's what we've gotter do. Save the country from the foreign enemies."

His faithful band waved their bows and arrows and cheered enthusiastically.

At first all went well. The Bow and Arrow Army practised diligently under William's leadership. They set up a target on a tree, stood in a long line one behind another, and as each came to the front on the word of command from William shot at the target, while the result was noted on a slate by Ginger. So far so good. But the archers with the perversity of human nature soon began to grow tired of it. They weren't content to stand in a row, step forward at William's word of command, shoot, and have the result noted on a slate by Ginger. It was all right just at first, but after an hour or so it became boring. True, the small boy who had challenged the historical truth of William's reference to Napoleon introduced a diversion by shooting William calmly and deliberately by a well aimed arrow in the middle of his stomach and running off, leavingWilliam writhing in agony on the ground. William, however, quickly recovered and was on the point of furiously pursuing his assailant when he was held back by Ginger who pointed out, truly enough, that if William were to leave them the bored archers would probably straggle off to other diversions. So William, ever an opportunist, turned the incident to account. He made another speech.

"Soldiers," he said. "You can jus' see from me being nearly killed then, what a deadly weapon a bow'n arrer is. That's what you've gotter do to the foreign enemies of the country, hit them in the stomach nearly killin' 'em like what John Francis did me. And," he ended simply, "when I catch John Francis I'll jolly well *show* him."

The archers, because cheering is a change from shooting at a target, cheered.

But the fact remained that the archers were growing bored. They preferred William as leader of lawless expeditions to William as Commander-in-Chief of a disciplined band of archers. Shooting at a target is thrilling enough for the first day, becomes less thrilling on the second and is boring in the extreme on the third. None of them dared to vary the monotony as had John Francis by shooting William. John Francis, it transpired, had acted thus quite safely in the knowledge that he was going away the next day on a fortnight's visit to an aunt, and it was a known fact that no insult ever lived in William's memory for longer than a week. William's life was too full to admit of his cherishing vengeance against anyone for longer than a week.

* * *

The scarecrows were William's idea. It was indeed such an idea as could have been no one's but William's. William realised that his band of warriors was growing daily more listless and discontented, that it was held together solely by the hope—daily diminishing—that something exciting really was going to happen soon, and they only did not desert in a body because they were afraid of finding afterward that they had missed an adventure.

So William thought of the scarecrows.

He realised that a target lacked human interest and he realised that in almost every neighbouring field stood a fairly lifelike scarecrow which might well serve to represent the foreign enemy to whose destruction he had so often urged his gallant band. Moreover all the fields were "trespass fields," and between William and the neighbouring farmers there waged a deadly feud which would lend to the expedition that element of lawlessness and adventure without which William as well as the archer band was feeling the whole thing to be rather flat.

Upon hearing this the archer band brightened perceptibly and set off behind their leader lovingly fingering their bows and chanting joyous songs of battle. The adventure did not disappoint them. They had a glorious day, a day that glowed brightly in their memories for many months. They surrounded every scarecrow in every field and shot at it with bow and arrow till it collapsed realistically and blood-curdingly into a heap on the ground. When the result did not take place quickly enough, they hastened it by a few discreetly placed stones. A scarecrow, as an enemy, possesses the supreme advantage (to its assailant) of not being able to do anything back. From two or three of the fields they were chased by irate farmers which gave the game the piquant edge of excitement they had all hoped for.

William would have liked his men to shoot at the farmer enemy as they retreated but even he had to admit that this was more difficult than it sounds. He tried it, hit Ginger by mistake and fell over a ploughed furrow at the same time. William had never heard of the Parthians but if he had, would have had a deep, deep respect for them. They retired, however, fleetly and in good order, leaving none of their number in the hands of the enemy who finally gave up the chase, and purple-faced with breathlessness and fury, contented themselves with standing and shaking their fists at them till they were out of sight. It was altogether a glorious and thrilling day. But William realised with something of apprehension that it could not be repeated indefinitely. It was doubtful even whether it could be repeated once. The scarecrows were completely demolished and if new ones were set up it was pretty certain that they would be closely guarded. No, the band must not expect a day like this every day. They must be content with routine work for some time after this—with drilling and shooting at targets. Before they disbanded William delivered one of his stirring speeches.

"Now we've seen to-day," he said, "what we can do to a foreign enemy if one lands an' comes right into the middle of England. We can knock 'em to pieces same as we did the scarecrows," he ignored the convenient passivity of the scarecrow enemy which had assured the victory, and continued, "an' then if they start runnin' after us we can get out of their way same as we did out of Farmer Jenks' an' Farmer Hodges', and then when they're too tired to run any more, we can shoot at 'em again same as we could have done at Farmer Jenks an' Farmer Hodges if it hadn't been tea-time. An'—an' now we've gotter go on practising quietly for a bit so's to be ready, 'cause—'cause we never know when we'll wake up one mornin' an' find all the fields full of foreign enemies what have come over in the night."

The band of archers, inspirited by the events of the day, cheered enthusiastically.

* * *

The next morning William woke early and looked out of the window. His eyes opened wider and wider and wider. He rubbed them and looked again. It was true. The fields near the house were full of soldiers and tents. He dressed himself in a state of stupefied amazement. It had really happened. A foreign enemy had really crossed over in the night and had entrenched itself in the fields about his home. William descended to breakfast still feeling dazed.

"I say," he said, "there's soldiers. All over the field."

"It'll be the manœuvres," said his sister Ethel casually.

"How do you *know* it's the mou—what you said?" said William sternly. Ethel looked at him.

"There'd be a fortune," she said, "for anyone who would invent a hairbrush that would make a boy's hair look tidy."

"But they'd never use it even if anyone did," said William's mother gloomy.

William snorted and sat down before his porridge plate. That was just like his family. A foreign enemy only a few yards away and all they could talk about was his hair. Probably when the foreign enemy started shooting at them and killing them they'd still be going on at him about his hair or his face or something. Nothing—nothing—could ever stop them. Bitterly William wondered whether such people were worth saving.

After a hasty breakfast he hurried out to his archer band. He found them mildly excited.

"But they're English soldiers," said one with a certain disappointment in his voice. "I've heard 'em talkin' English."

"*Course* they talk English, silly," said William crushingly, "but that doesn't *prove* they're English. *Course* they taught 'em English before they brought 'em over. Do you think they'd bring 'em over talking foreign langwidges an' arousin' everyone's suspicions. *Course not. Course* they c'n talk English. I bet they saw you listening an' started talkin' English jus' so's not to arouse your suspicions." William had come across this phrase in a Secret Service story the night before and was proud of having an opportunity of using it, "but you go'n listen to them when they don't think anyone's listenin' an' I *bet* you'll find 'em talkin' foreign langwidges."

Obviously the majority of the Archer band was impressed by this. But one small doubting warrior piped up:

"Well, when I told my father this mornin' that I'd seen 'em, he said, 'Oh, yes. It'll be the manooverers'——or something like that—'an' I don't suppose they'll be here more than a day or two.' "

"Yes," said William excitedly, "that's *jus'* it. That's jus' what they *knew* people'd say. They come here dressed like English soldiers an' talkin' English so as not to arouse suspicion and they know that the English people'll jus' take for granted that they're English till they start fightin' 'em and then it'll be too late. English people are like that. They look out of their windows an' see a lot of soldiers in English clothes talkin' the English langwidge an' they say, 'Oh, yes, it'll be the——the—mooverers'—same as what George's father said, an' Ethel said, and they start talkin' about my hair jus' as if they weren't goin' to be killed the next minute."

"What does it mean?" piped up a small archer in the background.

"What does what mean?" said William to gain time.

"That word you said—Mooverers."

William cleared his throat.

"It's—it's a French word meanin' English Soldier,"

he said. His stern eye wandered among his Archers daring any of them to deny it. No one did deny it because everyone believed it implicitly.

"Well, that's wot I say," went on William relieved, "they knew that when English people saw they were dressed like English soldiers an' talkin' the English langwidge they'd say, 'Oh, they're jus' mooverers,' an' not to do anythin' to stop 'em. They'll stay here till they've learnt all about the country, then they'll conquer the village an' then they'll go on an' conquer all the rest of England. But—we've—gotter *stop* 'em."

The Archers waved their bows and arrows and cheered enthusiastically. This was better than practising at a target. This was better even than shooting scarecrows.

"Let's go now," said William and added cautiously, "jus' to have a look at 'em first. We mus' make plans careful before we start fightin' 'em."

The band of Archers marched joyously down the road still cheering and waving bows and arrows.

At the gate of the large field they stopped and gazed at the scene. There were small tents and big tents, and everywhere soldiers were hurrying to and fro or standing talking in groups.

"There's some officers in that tent," said William, "an' I bet if you went up to it you'd find 'em talkin' foreign langwidges."

"Well, go up to it an' see," challenged Ginger.

"All right, I will," said William promptly accepting the challenge.

Watched in a thrilled silence by his Archers he went further down the road till he was just behind the tent, then he wriggled through the hedge. William had through long experience brought wriggling through hedges to a fine art. Then he crawled up to the tent and daringly lifted it an inch or so, placing his ear to the aperture. Inside were two young officers. The first had just said:

"I saw this old man coming out of the 'Blue Boar' this morning." And just as William lifted the flap and applied his ear to it, the other was replying:

"*Honi soit qui mal y pense.*"

William replaced the flap, crawled back to the hedge and wriggled through to the road.

"They were talkin' foreign langwidges," he said excitedly, "foreign langwidges wot I couldn't understand a word of——"

The Archers cheered loudly. So stimulated were they by the prospect of adventure, that they would have been bitterly disappointed had William brought back any other report.

"Well, we've gotta make *plans*," said William, assuming a stern and thoughtful demeanour.

"'Sno good *rushin*' at 'em, straight away. There's more of them than what there is of us. We've found out—*I've* found out, I mean—that they're a foreign enemy. Well, we've gotter save the country from 'em. That's what we've gotter do. But it's no good *rushin'* at 'em before we've made plans. We've gotta make *plans* first. An' we've gotter be *cunnin*' as well as brave 'cause there's so many more of them than what there is of us. We've gotter find out first who's the head of 'em an' we've gotter do it without—without arousin' their suspicions."

The Archers cheered again lustily.

They would have cheered William now whatever he had said. The longed-for adventure had come. They were willing to trust themselves blindly and joyously to William's sole leadership. Ginger felt that William was having rather more than his fair share of the limelight.

"I'll find out who's the head of 'em," he offered. "I bet it's a dang'rous thing to do but I bet I do it all right."

The Archers cheered Ginger.

"I bet it's no more dang'rous than seein' if they were talkin' in foreign langwidges," challenged William.

Ginger's proud spirit had been assuaged by the Archers' cheers. He felt that he could afford to be generous.

"No, it's just about the same," he conceded.

He wriggled through the hole which had been left in the hedge by the passage of William's solid body and began to creep very cautiously along the tents, peeping under each to see their interior. At one he evidently made a discovery of a sensational nature. He turned round, made excited but incomprehensible signs to the Outlaws who were watching over the hedge, then began to crawl back. He plunged through the hole and began at once.

"I've found the head of 'em. He's a big fat man with a red face an' a white moustache an' he's sittin' at a table lookin' at a map."

"Well, that *proves* it," said William equally excited, "that *proves* it. If he wasn't foreign he wun't need to be lookin' at a map, would he? If he was really English like what they pretend to be he wun't need to be lookin' at a map of England. He'd've done England at school in Geography."

The Archers agreed that the logic of this was unassailable.

William continued:

"Well, now that's the first thing we've gotter do. We've gotter take his map off him. I said it was no use *rushin'* at 'em an' we'd gotter be cunnin'. Well, that's the first cunnin' thing we've gotter do. We've gotter take his map off him an' then you see he won't know what to

GENERAL BRISTOW RECEIVED THE FULL FORCE OF WILLIAM'S BULLET-HEAD IN HIS STOMACH.

do or where he is or anythin'."

"Well," said Ginger hastily, "I've done enough findin' out about who he is. I'm not goin' to take his map off him."

"No," said William, "it's time Douglas did something."

The Archers cheered this.

It was well known that Douglas did not care to expose himself unnecessarily to danger. But Douglas received the suggestion with stoic courage. Despite his preference for a quiet life, Douglas was no coward.

THE ARCHERS, CROUCHING IN THE DITCH, LOOKED ON, HORROR-STRICKEN.

"All right," he said resignedly, "jus' tell me how to do it, an' I'll do it."

But the discussion was interrupted by the sight of the big fat man with the red face and white moustache emerging from his tent, map in hand.

"There he is!" hissed Ginger. "Din' I *tell* you? Map'n all!"

With eyes starting out of their heads the Archers watched the progress of the red-faced warrior as he came slowly down the field his eyes still fixed on the map outspread in his hands.

"Wonder what he's thinkin' about," said Ginger.

"Whatever he's thinkin' about," said William knowingly, "I bet he's thinkin' about it in a foreign langwidge."

The fat, red-faced man was coming to the gate of the field. His eyes still fixed on the map, he came out into the road.

The Archers, looking round for a hiding-place, saw none but the ditch into which they hastily precipitated themselves. The man came slowly down the road, still looking at the map. He passed the Archers crouching in the ditch. The sight of the enemy thus within his grasp was too much for William. Without waiting to consider or reason William acted.

General Bastow, walking peaceably down the road studying his map as he went, was amazed to see a boy suddenly scramble up out of the ditch by the roadside. A moment later he was still more amazed to receive the full force of the boy's bullet-head in his stomach, and to be forced by its sheer iron weight into a sitting posture in the dust. For a moment physical agony blinded him to everything but the outrage committed by that dastardly boy upon his digestive organs. Then his vision cleared. He found his map gone and a boy disappearing on the horizon. It was not General Bastow's habit to receive any outrage sitting down (except as in this case inadvertently). With a roar of fury he set off in pursuit, less in order to recover his map (of which he had other copies) than in order to inflict condign punishment upon the person of his assailant. But it was not for nothing that William was pursued regularly and unavailingly by all the local farmers. William's life had perforce been largely spent in throwing off pursuers. When General Bastow, plum-coloured and panting, had reached the cross-roads, there was no sign of William anywhere. It seemed futile to continue the pursuit, so the elderly warrior, panting and rumbling like a threatening volcano, returned slowly back along the road to the gate, which led into the field, and back into his tent. When he had finally disappeared, still rumbling furiously, into his tent, the Archers scrambled out of the ditch in an awe-struck silence and went towards the cross-roads where William had vanished.

There they saw William emerging, jaunty and unshaken, from behind a hayrick in a neighbouring field, carrying the map. He joined them on the road.

"Well," he chuckled, "*now* they'll be in a nice fix. They jolly well won't know what to do without the map. They won't know where they are or anythin'. I say"—with a reminiscent chuckle—"din't he go down with a flop?" Then with his own inimitable swagger: "My head's jolly strong. I bet there's jolly well no one I can't knock over with my head."

"What'll we do next?" said Ginger joyfully.

"Oh, jus' watch 'em for a bit," said William, "they won't know what to do without their map."

Next day every movement of the innocent company of territorials was interpreted by William as one of utter bewilderment and despair.

"Look at 'em, marchin' down there, cause that's where they saw me go off with the map an' they're tryin' to find it. They dunno what to do without it. Look at that one goin' into the village. He's going' to try'n buy another map an' he won't be able to 'cause they don't keep 'em. Look at that one postin' a letter. He's writin' off to the foreign country they come from to tell 'em that they've had the map took and to ask 'em what to do."

The great discovery was when he found a company of them digging a trench, at the end of the field.

"Look at 'em. They're givin' up tryin' to conquer England now they've had their map took off them an' they daren't go home by ship, same as they came, because they know now that someone knows about 'em with getting their map stole—so look at 'em. I bet they live at the other side of the world an' they're tryin' to dig themselves through back to their homes, you know, 'cause of the world bein' round like what they say it is in geography."

The Archers were so pleased with his idea that they cheered again lustily. Its only drawback was that few of them had really in their hearts ever subscribed to the theory that the earth is round. As Douglas said—when they began now to discuss the idea afresh:

"Stands to reason, dun't it, that folks can't walk about upside down like flies. They'd drop off the earth altogether. Even if they tried holdin' on by trees an' things they'd be sure to drop off in the end. Ships couldn't stay in the sea either. They'd drop out."

"And the sea cun't stay there neither," said Ginger, elaborating the theme. "You can't have water stayin' in a place upside down without anythin' to keep it in. It'd spill out."

"Well, what're we going' to do about this foreign army?" said an Archer who was not interested in the problematical shape of the earth.

"Jus' wait an' watch 'em for a bit still," said William. "We've got their map. They can't do anythin' without their map."

But by the end of the next day both William and his Archers had tired of waiting and watching.

They felt that the time was ripe for some decisive coup, and so they met in William's back garden to decide what form exactly the coup should take. William led the discussion.

"I votes," he said, "that we get the general man away from them somehow. Then when we attack them they'll have no one to tell'm what to do. They'll be without a leader an' we'll easy be able to put 'em to flight."

"Yes, but *how'll* we get the ole general away from them?" demanded the Archers.

"Well, we'll talk about that now," said William.

So they talked about that.

* * *

The next evening was the last evening of the manœuvres and there was a relaxed atmosphere about the camp. General Bastow set off to dine with an acquaintance who lived at the further end of the village, though the General wasn't quite sure where, as he'd never visited him before at home. Dusk was falling as he walked along the road. He had been terribly bored by the manœuvres and he still hadn't forgotten that brutal attack perpetrated upon him in broad daylight by that dastardly young ruffian. He was certain that his liver had never been the same since. He still had hopes of meeting that young ruffian face to face. He'd never come across a place with so many boys in it. Crowds of boys seemed to have been watching the camp ever since they settled there, peeping over the hedge, following men and officers about. He was rather short-sighted, and he hadn't had time to look for that young ruffian again, but he'd know him if he saw him. He turned a corner of the road and suddenly came across a small boy crying bitterly. It was the youngest Archer, but the General, of course, could not know this, nor could the General know that the whole body of Archers was concealed in the muddy ditch, watching the encounter. The General did not like small boys, but he felt that he could not pass by a small boy in such deep distress without some offer of assistance.

"Well, well, well," he bellowed irritably, "what's the matter with you, my little man?"

"I'm lo—o—o—o—ost!" sobbed his little man.

"Oh, nonsense! nonsense!" boomed the General. "Nonsense! We'll soon find your home for you!"

"T—thank you," sobbed his little man, slipping his hand confidently in his. "T—thank you."

The General had not quite bargained for this. He had not meant to spend his evening finding a home for a lost boy, but fate seemed to have thrust the situation upon him.

"Where do you think you live, my little man?" he said testily.

"D—down this road, I think," sobbed his little man.

In the gathering dusk he led his rescuer down the road.

"Will you recognise the house when you see it?" said the General.

"Y—yes, I think so," sobbed the youngest Archer.

"Well, stop crying, my good child, stop crying. Try to be a man. Crying won't do any good."

The youngest Archer stopped crying. He was glad to be told to stop crying. It is quite easy to sob convincingly for a minute or two but difficult to continue it indefinitely. He was afraid that his performance was beginning to lack realism. At each house along the road the General said, "Do you think you live here, my little man?" and his little man said with a break in his voice of which he was secretly proud. "No—no. N—not here." Till they got to the large house at the end of the road, then, when the General said, "Do you live here, my little man?" the youngest Archer said, brightly, "Why, yes, I think—I *think* it's here."

They entered the wrought iron gates together, and walked half way up the drive. Then the youngest Archer gently withdrew his hand and disappeared in the dusk. The General stood gazing around, his eyes and mouth wide open. The child had vanished as completely as if the earth had opened to swallow him up. Behind him he heard a clang of metal as the iron gates swung to. As he was standing there, amazed and indecisive, the front door opened and a voice said:

"That you, General?"

With relief the General recognised the voice of the friend with whom he was going to dine.

"Found your way to the house all right?" went on the friend.

"Well, a curious chance led me here," said the General, "as a matter of fact, I'd no idea it was your house till you spoke. A little boy who said he was lost—but he was probably playing a trick on me, the young ruffian. All boys are the same. Why, only the other day on the main road in broad daylight——"

Talking volubly he entered the hall with his host who shut the front door behind him.

When the General and the realistically sobbing youngest Archer had turned the bend of the road, the main body of Archers with their bows and arrows climbed out of the ditch and clustered round William.

"Well," said William, "I mus' say he did that jolly well—*jolly* well—— Now let's sep'rate. Ginger an' Douglas and half of you go after them an' me'n' the others'll go back an' charge the soldiers an' with him not bein' there they won't know what to do, an' they'll have no one to lead 'em. Come on!"

With a flourish he led his half army away and Ginger and his little band set off cautiously down the road in the wake of the General and the youngest Archer.

Soon they saw the youngest Archer come out of the gates, shut them behind him, and run excitedly down the road to meet them.

"I've shut him in," he said in a shrill whisper, "he's in all right."

They approached the iron gate and clustered around it, watching and listening. All was as still and silent as it had been when the youngest Archer left it. He could not know, of course, that he had led the General to his host nor that in that brief interval during which he ran to greet and report to his friends, the General had been received and admitted by the master of the house. They gazed and listened. All was still—all was silent—and it was growing dark.

"He's creepin' about the garden, I bet," said the youngest Archer, "tryin' to find a way out—— Look, I believe I c'n see him. Over there."

The more imaginative of the Archers said that they thought they could see him too.

"Well, half of us'll stay here guardin' this gate," said Ginger, "an' shoot him if he tries to come out, an' half go round to the back gate, an' guard that an' shoot him if he tries to come out. He won't *dare* to try'n take refuge in the house, 'cause it's Mr. Hunter's, an' he's a magistrate an' he'd know at once that he was a foreign enemy an' put him in prison. He'll either stay hidin' in the garden or else try'n' get out of this gate when we'll shoot him or else try'n' get out of the other gate when the others'll shoot him."

The others had already gone round to the side gate. Ginger and his little band pressed their noses against the wrought iron and gazed intently into the garden.

It was a windy night and black shadows moved with the swaying trees.

"Look, there he is," Ginger would say, "crouchin' down there! Look! He moved! D'you see!"

The Archers saw. With every minute that passed their imaginations grew keener and there was not one of them who did not distinctly see the dark shadow of General Bastow, creeping round the corners of the house and beneath the trees.

"He's gettin' desperater an' desperater," said Ginger, "he daren't go in 'cause he knows it's a magistrate livin' there, an' he daren't come out 'cause he knows we're waitin' to shoot him, an' he's jus' creepin' about gettin' desperater an' desperater."

It happened that in Mr. Hunter's garden was a pond much frequented by frogs. Suddenly through the night air came the sound of a frog's croak—then another —then another.

"Listen to him moanin' an' groanin'," interpreted Ginger, "gettin' desperater an' desperater."

There came the sound of a splash as a frog jumped into the pond and then silence.

"He's drowned himself," said Ginger in an awe-struck voice. "He's got desperater an' desperater till he's drowned himself."

There was another silence.

"He must have," said Ginger. "I don't see him creepin' about anywhere now, do you?"

The Archers didn't.

"Let's go'n' look," said a specially bold one.

They opened the gate cautiously and crept up the drive past the house to the pond. It was perhaps as well that they could not see through the dining-room blind the figure of their supposed victim sitting at a table, stout and red-faced as ever, eating and drinking heartily.

They clustered round the pond. Dark shadows lay at the bottom of it.

"I can see his dead body," said Ginger, "can't you? Over there. Under that tree. Right at the bottom."

The more imaginative Archers said they could see his dead body quite plainly. The less imaginative ones said that they thought they could.

"Well, we'd better go," said Ginger. "Now he's drowned hisself there's no use stayin' here keepin' guard. Let's go over the side gate an' go'n' help William."

* * *

Meanwhile William and his band had walked back to the field where the "foreign enemy" was still entrenched. Just behind the trench was the high wall which bounded a garden belonging to Miss Milton, an inveterate enemy of William's. But—fortunately for William—Miss Milton was away on her holiday and a caretaker occupied the house. William had little fear or respect for caretakers. He knew by long experience that they spent most of their time sleeping, were generally deaf and short-sighted and always short-winded. Heartened by this thought he collected and addressed his followers.

"*Now's* the time for us to attack 'em," he said flourishing his bow and arrows in a warlike manner. "*Now's* the time, while they haven't got their leader to tell 'em what to do. We'll go into Miss Milton's garden—careful, 'cause the old woman mightn't be asleep, but anyway she's sure to be deaf so it'll be all right. We'll climb up behind the wall an' lean over an' attack 'em with the bow an' arrers an' I bet you—I jolly well bet you *anythin'* you like that we put 'em to flight."

The Archers cheered in shrill excitement and marched off gaily in their leader's wake. William knew the best hole through the hedge into Miss Milton's garden. William knew the best holes through the hedges into most of his neighbours' gardens. This was not unnatural as most of them had been made by the frequent furtive passage of William's body. The other Archers followed less nimbly being less accustomed than their leader to such means of entrance. In the garden William stood and looked about him. All was silent and empty. There was not even a serpent in the garden in the shape of a gardener. And the windows at the back of the house were reassuringly blank. No suspicious caretaker's face was visible at any of them. William heaved a sigh of relief.

"*That's* all right," he said to his army. "Now come along—*creep*—to the bottom where the wall is."

They crept to the bottom of the garden, William creeping at their head. They imitated faithfully William's manner of creeping, but none of them approached William's creeping form. William was justly proud of his creeping. Not for nothing had he practised being a Red Indian and a robber chief and a cinema villain painstakingly and for many years. He had brought creeping to a fine art. The finest villain on the cinema stage might have learnt something from William's creeping. It was not perhaps a very unobtrusive mode of procedure but it was dramatic. He suited his expression to his walk and assumed an air of furtive cunning. So wrapt up was he in fulfilling his rôle of creeper to his own satisfaction that it was not till he reached the bottom of the garden that he realised that the wall was too high for them and that they could not possibly see over it, much less launch an attack from the top of it. The other Archers were taken aback, but William assumed his stern frown of leadership.

"We'll jus' have to get somethin' to stand on," he hissed in a dramatic whisper.

A small Archer attempted a cheer but was muffled and cuffed by an older one.

So they set about finding something to stand on. Under William's direction, and still creeping with melodramatic furtiveness to and fro, they fetched a table from a summer-house and put upon it a row of large plant pots upside down. As this did not hold them all, others moved forward a cucumber frame, stood it up sideways and balanced plant pots upon it. Then laboriously and, miraculously, without accident, they mounted the precarious erection and peeped cautiously over the top of the wall. Yes, the soldiers were still in the trench below them.

"Get your bows an' arrers ready," hissed William.

They got them ready as best they could, holding on to the wall with one hand while the erection of table and

"ONE, TWO, THREE—*FIRE!*" SAID WILLIAM, THEY FIRED.

cucumber frame and plant pots rocked beneath them.
"One, two, three—*fire!*" said William.
They fired.
It is one thing to stand on firm ground and take careful aim at a target affixed to a tree near you and quite

THE SOLDIERS SWARMED UP OUT OF THE TRENCH AND BEGAN TO RUSH ACROSS THE FIELD.

another to shoot over the top of a wall on to which you have to hold with your chin while an unsteady erection of plant pots and cucumber frame rocks beneath you. Most of the arrows went rather wild. But it happened that as the *grande finale* of the manœuvres the soldiers were practising an "over the top" charge out of the trench and across the field, and just as William's band shot their arrows the officer gave the signal to charge. The soldiers swarmed up out of the trench and began to rush across the field.

"We've put 'em to flight," roared William triumphantly, "we've p——"

But at this point the whole erection of plant pots, table and cucumber frame collapsed with a terrific clatter of breaking glass and pots. Shaken and apprehensive the Archers picked themselves up from the débris. Their apprehensions were not unfounded for immediately the kitchen door burst open and caretaker and gardener rushed out in avenging fury. The Archers, leaving their weapons ignominiously behind in the enemies' territory, scrambled precipitately through the hedge and were not a moment too soon. In fact the gardener seized the foot of the last Archer, who, with great presence of mind, wriggled his foot out of his shoe and, leaving his shoe in the gardener's hand, fled after the others down the road pursued by the shoe which the gardener flung after them, and which hit William neatly on the head. William was just about to throw it back and see if he could hit the gardener equally neatly on the head when its owner, who had been trying to invent a plausible explanation of its absence for his mother, snatched it from William's hand and put it on as he ran. The Archers did not dare to go down the road again towards the field where the irate gardener and caretaker presumably awaited them. So they marched down the road where they had left Ginger and his band, chanting pæans of victory. It was almost dark when they met Ginger and his band. They also were coming down the road chanting pæans of victory.

"We put 'em to flight," yelled William as soon as he caught sight of his friend.

"He's drowned hisself," yelled Ginger joyously.

They met and began excitedly to exchange reports.

"We just fired once," said William, "an'——"

"We shut the gate on him," said Ginger, "an'——"

"They went dashin' out of their hole terrified an'——"

"He went moanin' an' groanin' about the garden——"

"Simply *terrified*——"

"Gettin's desperater an' desperater."

"An' went tearin' away over the field."

"An' at last went an' drowned himself in a pond. . . ."

"We saw 'em *tearin'* away over the field."

"We heard a big splash and then saw his dead body in the pond an'——"

The Archers would have liked to have gone back to the field to see whether they were any traces of the routed enemy, but the thought of the caretaker and gardener, who probably still lay in wait for them with hostile intent, deterred them.

"We'd better not go back," said William, "they may've left bombs or—or snipers or somethin', but," he ended impressively, "I can jolly well tell you that there won't be *one* of 'em left to-morrow mornin'. They'll all go back home in their ships to-night."

And William was right in the first part of his prophecy. There was not one of them left in the morning. They had, as originally arranged, departed with praiseworthy dispatch and smartness in the early hours of the morning.

* * *

It was the next week and they were in William's back garden. William was still discussing the affair. The other Outlaws were beginning to get rather bored with the airs William put on about it. William seemed not to have stopped talking about it since it happened, and his boasting grew more unbearable every day.

"I oughter have a statchoo put up to me," he said. "I did it. It was all my idea. I've saved the country an' conquered a foreign enemy an' I oughter have a statchoo put up to me."

"Oh, shut up," said Ginger, "so ought I too, anyway, an' anyway I'm jolly tired of it an' let's go fishin' again."

"All right," said William, taking up the stick which bore a bent pin attached to it by a length of damp string. "All right. I don't mind. But wot I say is that I ought to have a statchoo put up to me for savin' the country. Yes, you ought to, too," he concluded hastily as Ginger began to speak, "you ought to, too, but I oughter have the biggest one because it was my idea anyway. I oughter be put up on a tall piller like Nelson. I ought——"

He stopped abruptly and stood as if petrified, his eyes staring in horror and amazement at a figure which was just coming in at the front gate.

General Bastow had returned after the manœuvres to spend a few days with his friend, Mr. Hunter, had met Mr. Brown there and had to-day been invited to the Browns' to lunch. William did not know this. Ginger and Douglas were equally petrified. The three of them stood transfixed with horror—eyes and mouths open wide. The visitor strode jauntily up to the front door. He did not see the three boys who were crouching behind the bushes.

William recovered from his stupor first. He turned to Ginger and hissed:

"Thought you said he'd drowned himself . . . thought you said you'seen his dead body."

Ginger's face was pale with horror.

"I did," he gasped, "I did honest. This must be his ghost."

"It can't be," said Douglas. "You can't see through it."

"You c-can't always see through them," said Ginger faintly.

"Dun't *look* like a ghost," said William grimly.

"It *mus'* be," said Ginger recovering gradually his normal manner. "It mus' be. I tell you I *sor* his dead body in the pond. He's haunting us 'cause we made him kill himself same as you said you'd haunt the man what nearly killed you with a motor car. I bet you *anythin'* that if you went up an' gave him a good hit the hit'd go right through him."

General Bastow had reached the front door and rung the bell. He stood there twirling his white moustaches still unaware of the three boys behind him.

"All right," said William, "go'n' do it. Go'n' give him a good hit and see if it goes through him."

"All right, I will," said Ginger unexpectedly.

Ginger had been so convinced that the black shadow at the bottom of the pond was General Bastow's dead body that he had no doubt at all that this apparition was General Bastow's ghost come back to haunt him. He had decided to show it once for all that he was not afraid of it. *He* would jolly well teach it to come haunting *him*.

Before either William or Douglas could stop him he had crept up behind the gallant warrior and dealt him a sound punch in the small of his back. The General started round, purple-faced and snorting with anger. The impact of his fist with the solid flesh of the General had convinced Ginger at once that this was no ghostly visitant from another world, and panic-stricken he had darted off into the bushes like a flash of lightning. Douglas, with admirable presence of mind, had followed him, and when the General turned, purple-faced and snorting, only William was there standing behind him, rooted to the spot in sheer horror. And at that moment William's father opened the door. The General pointed a fierce finger at William.

"Th-a-t boy's just hit me," he spluttered, going a still more terrific purple.

At this monstrous accusation the power of speech returned to William.

"I d-didn't," he gasped, "Ginger did. Ginger hit you b-because he thought you were a ghost."

The enormous figure of the General seemed to grow more enormous still and his purple face more purple still. His eyes were bulging.

"Thought I was a g—— Thought I was a *what?*"

"A ghost," said William.

"A GHOST?" roared the General.

"Yes, a ghost," said William; "he thought he'd drowned you and you'd come back to haunt him."

"He thought—WHAT?" bellowed the General.

"He thought he'd drowned you and you'd come back to haunt him. He was hitting you to see if the hit would go through you."

The General stared back at him and stared and stared. And a memory came back to him—a memory of a dusty road, a bullet-head in his stomach and an unavailing pursuit. He looked as if he were going to have an apoplectic fit. He pointed a trembling finger at William.

"Why—*you're* the boy," he sputtered, "who——"

William's father intervened quietly.

"Yes," he said. "Come and tell me what he did indoors."

* * *

It was evening. William and Ginger and Douglas sat gloomily in William's back garden.

"That's all one gets," said William bitterly, "for

savin' one's country. That's all one gets for puttin' a foreign enemy to flight. Bein' treated like that. Oh, no, no one believes me, do they? Oh no. They'll believe any lies any foreign enemy tells them, won't they? but not me, not me what's saved the country. They won't believe anythin' I say. Oh, no. I can save the country from a foreign enemy, but *that* doesn't make any difference. Oh, no. They won't listen to a word I say. Oh, no. But they'll listen to a foreign enemy all right. Oh, yes. Well, I've jolly well finished with 'em and *now—now*"—impressively he brought out his terrible threat—"if they came to me on their knees *beggin'* to put up a statchoo to me. I wouldn't let 'em."

Chapter 4

William—The Money Maker

The Outlaws stood around and gazed expectantly at William.

"Well, where're we goin' to get 'em?" said Ginger.

"Buy 'em," said William after a moment's deep thought.

There was another silence. The solution was felt to be unworthy of William.

"*Buy* 'em!" echoed Douglas in a tone that expressed the general feeling, "*buy* 'em! Who's got any money?"

This question being unanswerable remained unanswered. It was a strange fact that the Outlaws never had any money. They all received pocket money regularly and they all received the usual tips from visiting relatives, but the fact remained that they never had any money. Most of it, of course, went in repairing the wreckage that followed in the train of their normal activities—broken windows, shattered greenhouse frames, ruined paintwork and ornaments which seemed to the Outlaws deliberately to commit self-destruction on their approach. As William frequently remarked with deep bitterness:

"Meanness, that's what it is. Meanness. Anythin' to keep the money themselves 'stead of givin' it to us.

Seems to me they go about makin' things easy to break so's they c'n have an excuse for keeping it themselves instead of givin' it us. *Meanness*. That's what it is."

The parents of the Outlaws who formed a sort of unofficial Parents' Union and generally worked in concert had evolved the system of fines—one penny for being late to a meal, a half-penny for dirty hands at meals and a farthing for not scraping their boots before coming into the house (merely wiping them was insufficient. The Outlaws always brought in with them the larger part of the surrounding countryside). What was salvaged from the general wreckage of their finances caused by this ruthless tyranny seldom passed the test of the close proximity of Mr. Moss' sweet shop with its bottles of alluring sweets and its boxes of less lasting but more intriguing chocolate "fancies".

"*Buy* 'em," echoed Henry with deep feeling. "What're we to buy 'em with? There's *laws* to stop people takin' money off other people, but my father"—with heavy sarcasm—"don't seem to have heard of 'em. He'll be getting into trouble one of these days takin' other people's money off them. He's startin' with me, what he thinks can't do anythin' back, but he'll be going' on to other people soon like what the Vicar said people always do what begin pickin' an' stealin' in little things an' then he'll be gettin' into trouble. Takin' sixpence off me jus' for bein' late for a few meals! An' then they keep sayin' why don't we *save*. Well, what *I* say is why don' they give us somethin' to *save*, 'fore they start goin' on an' on at us for not savin'. Not that I b'lieve in savin'," he added hastily, "I don' b'lieve in savin' an' I never have b'lieved in savin'. Money isn't doing' any good to anyone—not while you're savin' it. I think it's *wrong* to save money. Money doesn't do any good to you or to anyone else. Not while you're savin' it.

It's kinder to help the poor shop people by spendin' money at their shops. How'r the poor people in shops goin' to live if all the people save their money an' don't spend any of it? . . . Well, anyway that's what *I* think."

This was for Henry an unusually long and an unusually eloquent speech. It showed that he had been stirred to the depth of his feelings. There was a moment's impressed silence. Then the others murmured in sympathy and Douglas said: "Let's go'n look at 'em again."

* * *

They were in the window of the little general shop at the other end of the village. . . . Three of them, beautiful in shape and strength and size and symmetry, with brass tops—cricket stumps. They were priced eight and sixpence.

"Golly!" said Ginger wistfully. "Just think of *playin'* with 'em!"

"You *can* get 'em cheaper than that," suggested Douglas tentatively, "you can get 'em for three and six. Smaller, of course, and not so nice."

The Outlaws, who were flattening their noses against the glass and gazing at the stumps like so many Moseses gazing at the Promised Land, treated Douglas' suggestion with contempt.

"Who'd want to play with cheap ones after seeing these ones?" said William sternly. "There's no *sense* in talkin' about *cheap* ones now we've seen these ones. I—I'd sooner go on playin' with the tree than play with *other* ones now we've seen these ones."

The Outlaws had these holidays developed a passion for cricket. They had, of course, partaken in the pastime in previous years, but listlessly and with boredom as in a pastime organised by the school authorities and therefore devoid of either sense or interest. Fielding had, of course, provided ample opportunity for studying the smaller fauna which infested the cricket pitch (last term Ginger had several times been hit squarely in the back while engaged in catching grasshoppers at mid-on), and batting was usually of short duration, but not until these holidays had the Outlaws regarded cricket as a game to be played for its own sake when not under the eye of Authority. The discovery was a thrilling one. The Outlaws in this as in everything threw moderation to the winds. They played cricket in season and out of season. They began the game before breakfast and continued it throughout the day with intervals for meals. They considered cricket far more enlivening when played with four players than when played with twenty-two. Ginger's elder brother gave them an old ball and Douglas had had a bat for a birthday present. Stumps they did not worry about. They chalked stumps on a tree trunk and played quite happily with them for a long time. But they found that stumps chalked on a tree trunk have their drawbacks, of which the chief one is that the bowler and batter are seldom agreed as to when one is hit. The Outlaws generally settled the question by single combat between batter and bowler, which at first was all right because the Outlaws always enjoyed single combats, but as the game itself became more and more exciting the perpetual abandoning of it to settle the score by single combat became monotonous and rather boring.

It was then that the Outlaws decided to procure stumps. Had they not happened to see the eight and six set all would have been well. They would have stuck sticks into the ground or scraped together enough money to buy an inferior set at one and eleven. But—not now. Now that they had seen the eight and six set of stumps, the set of stumps *de luxe*, the set of stumps with brass tops from the Land of the Ideal, they knew that all the savour would be gone from the game till they possessed them.

"Eight and six," said Douglas gloomily. "Well, we shall never get eight and six, so we may as well stop thinking of them, and just do the best we can with sticks."

This spiritless attitude irritated William.

"*Why* can't we get eight an' six?" he said. "Of course we c'n get eight an' six if we want it."

"All right," challenged Douglas, as irritated by William's attitude as William had been by his. "If you c'n get eight an' six, go an' *get* eight an' six."

"All right, I will," said William.

He hadn't exactly meant to say this, but the words were out so he accompanied them with a careless swagger.

They eyed him morosely and yet with a gleam of hope.

"Course you can't get eight an' six," they said. "How c'n you get eight an' six?"

William having taken up a position, however rashly, was not going to abandon it.

"P'raps *you* can't," he said kindly. "I daresay *you* can't, but if *I* want to get eight an' six I bet I c'n get eight an' six."

"Before to-night?" said Ginger. "You'll bring 'em here to-night?"

William was for a second taken aback by thus having the soaring flights of his fancy tied down to time and space.

He blinked for a moment, then recovering his swagger said:

"Course. You wait and see."

* * *

He walked home rather thoughtfully. Eight and six. The magnitude of the sum staggered his imagination. How could he get one and six or even sixpence, let alone eight and six? Not for the first time he regretted those rash impulses that always seemed to visit him at critical moments and make him undertake quite impossible tasks. The actual undertaking was, of course, a glorious moment—the careless swagger, the impression he gave himself as well as his audience of hidden resources, secret powers—almost of omnipotence.

But afterwards—and *eight and six!* William felt as helpless as if he had undertaken to provide a million pounds. He did not remember ever possessing as much money as eight and six. He did not remember ever knowing anyone who possessed as much money as eight and six. And yet—he knew that his prestige was at stake. With simple, touching faith the Outlaws were now looking to him to provide eight and six before to-night.

Up till now William had, owing to strokes of pure luck, always managed to make good his spectacular promises of the impossible, but this time he thought that he had met his Sedan. He did not think it in those exact words, of course, because he had not yet got to Napoleon. He was still laboriously and uninspiredly doing the Wars of the Roses. But he did think that he was in a beastly hole and he'd look a nice fool when he met them to-night with only the twopence-halfpenny which he might be able to extort from the boy next door, in exchange for a set of cigarette cards. (The boy next door never had more than twopence-halfpenny, and as he did not collect cigarette cards the exchange would have to be forcibly effected.) Looking round all his available resources. William did not see any prospect of anything except that possible twopence-halfpenny. His family, of course, was out of the question. His brother and sister always pretended that they had no money which, as William knew, was absurd, considering that they were grown up and had magnificent allowances and nothing to spend them on. It seemed to William one of the many ironies of fate that when you were young—say eleven—and had a lot of interesting things to buy, such as cricket bats and sweets and pistols and airguns and mouth organs, you had only a measly twopence a week, and when you were old—say eighteen like his brother—and had lost your taste for interesting things, they gave you shillings and shillings which you simply went and wasted on things like clothes and notepaper and suitcases and books (to quote a few recent instances of waste of money which William had noticed in the adult members of his family). It always made him feel bitter to see perfectly good money which might have been spent on cricket bats and sweets and pistols and air guns and mouth organs squandered on such things as clothes and notepaper and suitcases and books. His sister had particularly disgusted him only the other week by buying an expensive book of music. How much better and kinder it would have been, thought William, to buy the cricket stumps for him. . . .

His mother? His mother was softer hearted than any other member of his family (which in William's opinion was not saying much), but only yesterday he had inadvertently spilt boiling sealing-wax on the top of her polished writing-table while carrying on—without her knowledge—some private and highly interesting experiments with a sealing-wax set which she had won as a prize at a bridge drive. The set consisted of little balls of sealing-wax and a tiny saucepan in which to heat them over a little candle, and as soon as William saw it he knew that his spirit would have no rest till he had tried it. As he explained to her when she discovered the damage, he did not know that it was going to boil over on to her table like that. . . . He had made things worse by trying to get the mark out with ammonia because he had seen his mother the night before getting a stain out of his suit with ammonia.

His mother had covered up the mark by the simple expedient of putting the ink pot upon it and had agreed to say nothing about it to William's father, but William felt it was hardly a propitious moment for approaching her with a request for eight and sixpence. . . .

His father? . . . he hadn't yet paid for the landing window and his father was presumably still feeling annoyed about the cricket ball which had accidentally hit him yesterday evening when William was practising bowling in the garden. No: it would be little short of suicidal to approach his father for eight and six to-day and quite hopeless at any time. Extraordinary to think of the hundreds of pounds which must be wasted on quite useless things every year and no one would give him eight and six for a really necessary thing like cricket stumps. . . .

He wandered gloomily homeward. A youth with projecting teeth met him and gave him an expansive smile of greeting. William replied with his darkest scowl. He recognised the youth as Ethel's latest admirer and one of the most unsatisfactory admirers Ethel had ever had. He had given the youth every chance to buy his good graces, and the youth had not presented him with so much as a cigarette card. William, who did not believe in wasting efforts, had long since ceased to greet the youth with any attempt at pleasantness. Pleasantness to Ethel's admirers was in William's eyes a marketable quality and this youth had not seen fit to purchase it.

After turning to watch the youth out of sight and wasting upon the youth's unconscious back an exceptionally expressive grimace of scorn and ridicule, William continued gloomily to plod his homeward way.

On arriving home he first went up to his bedroom and carried out a systematic search of all his drawers and pockets. William was an incurable optimist and always hoped to find some day a forgotten coin in a pocket or a corner of a drawer. Ginger had once found a halfpenny in the pocket of a flannel suit he had not worn since the summer before, and ever after that all the other Outlaws had lived in hopes of doing the same thing. The search, however, proved in this case fruitless. It revealed only a rusty button and an old whistle which must have lost some vital part, for though William, temporarily forgetting the eight and six, expended a vast amount of wind and energy on it no sound of any sort resulted. Thereupon, purple in the face and breathless, he threw it indignantly out of the window. It seemed to him a typical example of fate's way of dealing with him. Even when he found an old whistle it hadn't any blow in it. . . .

Scowling bitterly and still trying to devise some method by which one might conjure eight and sixpence out of the void he descended to the garden.

* * *

In the garden he found his sister Ethel wearing a neat land girl's costume and weeding a bed. The Browns were temporarily without a gardener, and Ethel had undertaken the care of the garden till a new one should be engaged. She had done this chiefly because she had discovered how extremely fascinating she looked in a land girl's outfit. The land girl's outfit was partly responsible for the fatuous smile on the projecting teeth of the youth who had just left her. . . .

William watched her for a minute in silence. His thoughts were still bitter. Spending money on that old gardening suit that might have been used to buy the stumps. . . . His eye roved round the garden. . . . Spending money on spades and rakes and watering cans and seeds and flowers and things that didn't do any good to anyone . . . things that must have cost ever so many eight and sixes, and they wouldn't give him one little eight and six to buy a useful thing like cricket stumps.

Suddenly an inspiration visited him.

"Can I help you, Ethel?" he said with an ingratiating smile.

She looked up at him suspiciously, began a curt refusal, then stopped. She was growing tired of gardening. She was growing tired of her land girl's outfit. Its novelty had worn off and it was rather hot and stuffy. The youth with projecting teeth admired her in it intensely, but then she was growing tired of the youth with projecting teeth. She stood up and stretched.

"How much do you want for it?" she demanded brusquely.

She laboured under no delusions as to the disinterestedness of William's offers of help. She had known William too long for that.

"Sixpence an hour," said William daringly.

He never thought she'd give it him. But Ethel was sick of kneeling on the ground in the hot sun in a suit of clothes she was beginning to dislike, slaving for a lot of silly plants which didn't seem to look any better when she'd done with them.

"All right," she said.

William did a hasty sum. Eight and six. Two sixpences in a shilling. Twice eight are sixteen and the other sixpence seventeen. Seventeen hours. *Crumbs!*

"I meant a shilling," he said quickly.

"Well, you said sixpence and sixpence is all you'll get," said Ethel, unfeelingly.

"CAN I HELP YOU, ETHEL?" WILLIAM SAID, WITH AN INGRATIATING SMILE. ETHEL LOOKED UP AT HIM SUSPICIOUSLY.

William was not surprised. He hadn't really hoped for anything else from Ethel. Well, it would be a beginning . . . and perhaps when he'd got this bit of money something else would turn up.

"What d'you want me to do?" he said.

"Water the rose beds with the hose pipe and weed the bed on the lawn and pick a basket of strawberries for mother. *Pick*, not eat, remember."

William haughtily ignored the insult contained in the last sentence and mentally contemplated his directions with a professional air.

"Well," he said at last, "that'll take me a good many hours. I daresay that'll take me all the rest of to-day, late into the night an' most of to-morrow." He was struggling in his head with vast and complicated mental sums . . . hours into sixpences—sixpences into shillings. . . . She interrupted them.

"It oughtn't to take you more than two," she said. "Anyway I'm not paying you for more than two. It oughtn't really to take you one."

"*Well!*" said William in a tone of surprise and indignation, as if he was unable to believe his ears. "*Well!*"

But Ethel was already out of earshot. She was going to change the land girl's outfit (which she had finally decided was not really her style at all) for a dress of printed chiffon.

William stood and stared around the garden despondently. What was one shilling in eight and six? Then his ever ready optimism came to his aid. One shilling was better than nothing. . . . He might as well start on it. What had she said first? The hose pipe. . . . Well, it wouldn't be so bad. Quite apart from the shilling the hose pipe always had its bright side. . . . Normally William was forbidden the use of the hose pipe. Even Ethel wouldn't have told him to use the hose pipe if she hadn't been in a state of weary disgust with gardening in general and her land girl's suit in particular. William fitted on the hose pipe nozzle and turned on the tap. He had no thought in his mind except the watering of the rose beds as directed, and the earning of his shilling.

It was sheer bad luck that just at the critical moment when he was about to deluge the rose bed he suddenly caught sight of his inveterate enemy, the next-door cat, silhouetted against the sky on the top of the wall. William did not stop to reason. He acted on the overpowering impulse of the moment. He turned the full flow of the hose pipe on to the person of his enemy. His enemy nimbly evaded it and it flowed in a pellucid unbroken fountain over a wall into the next garden. There came a shrill scream.

"The brute! He's soaked me!" a voice shrilled.

"Me too!" screamed another. "Oh, the brute! Who was it? I'm soaked."

"It must be that awful boy next door."

"Look over the wall and see if you can see him. Stand on the chair!"

After a few minutes' interval an irate and dripping head appeared over the wall and looked around for William. It did not see William, however. William, crouching behind the rain tub, was quite hidden from view. It saw, however, the hose pipe flung upon the ground and discharging its full force down the garden path.

"It's him," said the voice. "I don't see him but I know it's him. He's left the thing there. Look! Pouring out. It must be him."

"Let's go straight in to change and then go and tell his father. I'm still soaked."

The head disappeared; the sound of indignant voices grew fainter; a distant door closed.

William emerged from behind the rain butt and hastened to turn off the tap and put away the hose pipe. . . . All that beastly cat's fault. Now he came to think of it hose pipes always had been unlucky for him. There'd been that little affair at the doctor's only a few months ago. . . .

Well, he'd better get on with the rest of it and try and

get the shilling safely before they were dry enough to come and see his father. What had she told him to do next? Weed the bed on the lawn. William promptly knelt down and weeded the bed on the lawn with commendable thoroughness. There was no doubt at all in William's mind as to what constituted a weed. In William's mind a weed was any plant he did not know the name of. William knew the names of very few plants. When he had finished weeding the bed contained a few straggling stocks and asters and one marguerite. By his side lay a pile of uprooted lobelias, petunias, calceolarias, veronicas and other plants. He carried these carefully to the rubbish heap, then gazed with pride at the bed on which he had been working.

"Looks a bit tidier now," he said.

Only one more thing to do. What was that? Oh, a basket of strawberries. He got a basket from the greenhouse and proceeded to the strawberry bed. He sat down there and a languorous content stole over him.

* * *

Ethel appeared dressed in the printed chiffon. She looked very dainty and bewitching. She'd decided to send the land girl's suit to the next parish jumble sale—it really wasn't her style. . . . William ought to have finished now. She'd give him his shilling and then she'd tell her father that she'd done what she'd said she'd do in the garden and she jolly well wouldn't offer to do any more. Anyway, a new gardener would be coming next week. . . . She suddenly stopped motionless, her eyes wide open in horrified amazement. The rose bed was still unwatered, but the garden path was completely swamped. Her eyes wandered slowly to the bed on the lawn which she had told William to weed. It was as William had left it—completely denuded except for half a dozen straggling plants whose presence only emphasised its desolation. There was no sign of William. Ethel went round to the kitchen garden. William was sitting on the path by the strawberry bed still in a state of languorous content. Ethel stared from the empty basket to the empty strawberry bed and from the empty strawberry bed to William's gently moving mouth.

"You *naughty* boy!" said Ethel. "You've *eaten* them, every one!"

William awoke with a start from his state of languorous content and looked at the basket and the strawberry bed. He was almost as amazed and horrified as Ethel.

"I say," he said. "I din't meant to eat 'em *all*. I din't honest. I only meant to try jus' one or two jus' to make sure they was all right before I started pickin' 'em. I—I expect really it's the birds that did it when they saw I wasn't lookin'. *Honest*, I don't think I could've eaten 'em all—I'm sure I only ate just a few—jus' to see they was all right."

Ethel's fury burst forth.

"I shan't give you any money and I shall tell father the *minute* he comes in."

This reminded William of something else.

"I say, Ethel," he said anxiously. "No one's—no one's been in to see father jus' lately, have they?"

"Oh," snapped Ethel. "Why?"

"No, nothin," said William. "I mean I jus' thought p'raps someone might be jus' sort of comin' to see him, that's all."

Ethel turned on her heel and walked away. Slightly to relieve his feelings William put out his tongue at her back. He might have known Ethel would let him slave for her for all this time and then not give him a penny. It was just like Ethel. He'd known her all his life and he might have known she'd play him a mean trick like that. Getting him to work like a nigger and promising him a shilling and then not giving him a penny jus' because—well jus' because of hardly anything.

A great despondency possessed William. He seemed to be farther off the eight and six than ever. . . . Ethel being Ethel would not be likely to forget to tell his father and presumably the recipients of the contents of the hose pipe were already drying themselves in preparation for their visit. . . . He was in for a rotten time. He wouldn't have minded if he'd got the eight and six. He wouldn't mind anything if he'd got the eight and six. He decided that it would be as well to leave the strawberry bed, so after carefully wiping his mouth to remove any chance stains, he wandered disconsolately round to the front of the house. His mother was coming out of the front door, dressed in her best clothes.

It struck Mrs. Brown that her younger son was looking rather pathetic. She was short-sighted and she often mistook William's expression of fury and disgust for one of pathos. It was a mistake which had often served William well.

"Would you like to come with me, dear?" she said pleasantly.

"Where to?" said William guardedly.

"To a nice little Sale of Work in Miss Milton's garden," said his mother. "I'm sure you'll enjoy it."

William was sure he wouldn't, but it occurred to him that he might as well be at Miss Milton's nice little Sale of Work as anywhere. Better than staying at home where his father and the next door neighbours might arrive any minute.

"A'right," said William graciously. "I don't mind."

"Very well, dear. I'll wait for you. Go and wash and brush yourself."

"I have washed and brushed myself," said William. "I did it specially well this morning to last the day."

"Well, it hasn't done, dear," said Mrs. Brown simply. "So go and do it again."

With a deep, deep sigh expressive of bitterness and disillusion and unexampled patience under unexampled wrongs, William went to do it again.

* * *

The first person he saw at the Sale of Work was Ethel in the printed chiffon accompanied by the young man with projecting teeth. William, who had detached himself from his mother, passed them without acknowledging them and hoped that they felt small. As a matter of fact they had not noticed him. He wandered about the garden. It might have been a more or less enjoyable affair for there were bran tubs and coconut shies and Aunt Sallies on a small scale—had William not been weighed down by his heavy financial anxieties. He was obsessed by the thought of the eight and six.

There simply didn't seem any way in the world of getting eight and six. . . .

He found his mother and assuming that expression that he found so useful in his dealings with her said: "Mother, please may I have a little money to spend here?"

His mother was obviously touched by his tone and expression, but after a brief inward struggle seemed to conquer her weaker feelings.

"I'm afraid not, William dear, because you know what your father said about the landing window last week. But I'll give you just one penny, because it's all in a good cause and I'm sure your father didn't mean when it was a case of charity. But not more than one penny."

So Mrs. Brown gave him a penny which he pocketed carefully as the nucleus of the eight and six.

Then he began to wander disconsolately round the grounds again. A small tent bearing the legend "Crystal Gazer" attracted his attention. He looked at it with interest for some time, then turned to a bystander.

"What's a Crystal Gazer?" he asked.

"A sort of fortune teller," answered the bystander absently.

A sort of fortune teller . . . perhaps a fortune teller might tell him how to get eight and six. . . . William went off to find his mother. She was serving at a stall. He assumed his pathetic expression and wistful voice again.

"Mother, please," he said. "May I have my crystal gazed?"

But Mrs. Brown was busy and the effect of William's pathetic expression and wistful voice was beginning to wear off.

"No dear," she said very firmly. "I don't believe in it. I think it very wrong to meddle with the future."

William walked back to the tent deeply interested. The fact that his mother considered it wrong invested it with a sort of glamour in his eyes, and "meddling with the future" sounded vaguely exciting. The tent was not opened yet, but was due to open in ten minutes. Already a queue of prospective clients was lined up before the doorway. William wandered round to the back of the tent. He had forgotten even the eight and six in a consuming curiosity about the crystal gazing. The back of the tent was quite deserted. Cautiously William descended to his hands and knees, held up the canvas and peeped underneath. Inside the tent was the young man with projecting teeth and a girl whom William recognised as the young man's sister. The young man was just giving her a paper.

WILLIAM LAY ON THE GROUND AND LISTENED.

"She doesn't know you're going to do it. does she?" the young man was saying.

"No. And I shall be wearing this veil. It quite hides my face."

"Well, just say to her what's on this paper, will you?"

"All right." The girl put the paper on the table and said, "Now do get out. I've got to start."

The young man got out and after a few minutes the queue began to enter one by one. William lay on the ground and listened beneath the canvas flap. He found it rather dull. When it was a girl the crystal gazer saw either a dark man or a fair man in the crystal and when it was a man the crystal gazer saw either a dark girl or a fair girl in the crystal. . . .

"I SEE SOMEONE," THE CRYSTAL GAZER SAID IMPRESSIVELY, "WHOSE LIFE IS CLOSELY BOUND UP WITH YOURS." "WHO IS HE?" SAID ETHEL, WITH INTEREST.

It was so dull that William was just going to abandon his post of eavesdropping when Ethel entered. He saw the crystal gazer move the paper on her table, concealed from Ethel by a book, so that she could read it.

"I see someone," she read impressively from the paper, "whose life is closely bound up with yours. At present you do not appreciate him. You are harsh and cold to him. But he has great qualities which you have not yet discovered. He is a far nobler character than you think."

"Who is he?" said Ethel, with interest.

"I will show you how to tell who he is," said the crystal gazer. "I can see him here. He is giving you a present. I can even see the time. It is just five minutes after you leave this tent. I see him again. He is sitting next to you at tea. I see him again. He is meeting you on your way home. He asks you a question. Let me tell you that the happiness of your whole life depends upon your saying 'yes'. That is all I have to tell."

Looking deeply impressed Ethel left the tent by the front.

Looking equally impressed William left the tent by the back.

It was exactly five minutes after Ethel left the tent when William, carrying a penny bag of monkey nuts, met the young man carrying a five-shilling bunch of roses and wearing a fatuous smile.

"You lookin' for Ethel?" said William.

"Yes."

"She's right over the other end by the gate," said William.

The young man hastened off towards the gate.

William went to his mother's stall where Ethel was helping and handed her the bag of monkey nuts.

"Here's a little present for you, Ethel," he said.

Suspiciously Ethel opened it. Ordinarily she would have accepted it either as a deliberate insult or as a feeble attempt to buy her silence about the hose pipe and the strawberries. But she looked at the clock. It was just five minutes after her departure from the crystal gazer's tent. . . .

She threw a bewildered glance at William's expressionless face and received the bag with a confused murmur. It was certainly curious, a present just five minutes after leaving the tent . . . someone she didn't appreciate. The young man did not find her till ten minutes afterwards and she was still puzzling so deeply over her mysterious present from William at the exact minute foretold by the crystal gazer that she hardly noticed the roses at all—merely murmured "thanks" and put them on the side table and went on thinking about William presenting her with a bag of monkey nuts at the exact minute foretold by the crystal gazer.

The young man was on the look-out when Ethel and Mrs. Brown went to the tea tent. He accompanied them, walking on the other side of Ethel, talking, and smiling amicably. William walked behind. They entered the tea tent. They approached the row of chairs. They began to sit down on three chairs, Mrs. Brown at one end, Ethel in the middle and—it wasn't till the young man was in the act of sitting down that he saw that William was on the seat. William was sitting between Ethel and him. Ethel was staring at William in amazement. William was gazing in front of him unperturbed and sphinxlike, as though in a trance. The young man asked William to change placed with him. William refused. He said that he'd better sit there so that he could pass things to his sister and his mother and Mrs. Brown said that that was very nice of him, and thought how William's manners were improving, and that she must remember to tell his father.

Ethel was very silent. She continued to gaze at William with mingled amazement and bewilderment and anxiety. The fortune teller had said "he"—William had given her a present and here he was sitting next to her at tea—most curious. She was so silent that the young man finally gave up all attempts to entertain her and contented himself with glaring balefully at William. William continued to gaze blankly in front of him as if unaware of their presence and to make a very good tea.

* * *

People were going home now. Mrs. Brown was staying to help dismantle the stalls but Ethel had set off home by herself. She was going the short cut home across the fields. She climbed over a stile. She saw the young man at the other end of the field standing by the further stile obviously waiting for her. She walked demurely and daintily towards him. Then suddenly as if he had sprung up from a ditch (which as a matter of fact he had) William appeared.

"Please, Ethel," he said meekly, "will you give me eight and six?"

She stared at him open-mouthed with amazement at the request—the cheek of it! And then her thoughts travelled suddenly back to the crystal gazer . . . "meet on your way home" . . . "request" . . . "happiness of your whole life depends upon your saying yes."

Ethel was superstitious. Dreadful things might happen to her if she refused and yet—*eight and six*. Still—no, she daren't refuse. *Anything* might happen to her if she refused. . . . Furiously she opened her purse . . . *eight and six*—it would only leave her a pound till the end of the month.

Angrily she flung the coins at William and walked on. She felt so angry that when she reached the young man at the further stile she walked straight past him without looking at him or answering him when he spoke to her. . . .

* * *

Mr. Brown sat in his chair in the drawing-room holding his head. On one side of him was Ethel and on the other side the ladies from next door. Ethel was feeling especially bitter at the thought of the eight and six. She had long ago repented of giving it to William. She'd never go to a crystal gazer again. She'd been an absolute idiot. It was all rubbish . . . making her give William eight and six. . . . She felt she could almost kill William. But as she couldn't do that she contented herself with expatiating on his horticultural failures.

"He hadn't *touched* the bed with it," she was saying.

"It *deluged* us," said the ladies from next door.

"He'd pulled up *everything*," said Ethel.

"Came over in a perfect fountain and *deluged* us," said the ladies next door.

"And he simply ate every one—every single one in the bed," said Ethel, "there wasn't *one* left."

"Must have been done deliberately," said the ladies next door, "it absolutely *deluged* us."

Mr. Brown removed his head from his hands.

"Where *is* he?" he groaned.

But no one knew where he was.

He was a matter of fact at the other end of the village. He was swaggering up to the Outlaws with the brand new eight and six stumps under his arm. The Outlaws were gaping at him stupefied with amazement and admiration.

"Said I'd get the money," said William airily, "so I—jus' got it. Thought I might as well get the things an' bring 'em along with me. Here they are."

It was a moment worth living for.

William felt that he really didn't care *what* happened to him after that.

Chapter 5

William—The Avenger

The Outlaws had noticed and disliked him long before the unforgivable outrage took place.

He had a tooth-brush moustache, a receding chin, an objectionable high-pitched laugh and a still more objectionable swagger. He admired himself immensely.

Somehow the Outlaws sensed trouble from him as soon as they saw him, even before they had found out anything about him. The Outlaws, of course, always made it their business to find out all about any strangers who appeared in the village. His name, they discovered, was Clarence Bergson, and he was staying at the Holdings, who were renting the Hall.

Now this was unfortunate because William liked the Holdings, or rather William liked Miss Holding, and for Miss Holding's sake accepted Mr. and Mrs. Holding—large and pompous and dignified, and disapproving of all small boys.

William admired Miss Holding because she was very young and very, very pretty and had a twinkle in her eye and a nice smile. He admired her in fact so much that when first he heard that Clarence Bergson was a friend of hers and staying at the Hall, he had been quite willing to overlook the receding chin and the high-pitched laughter and the objectionable swagger.

Clarence, however, rushed on to his doom. He began

by kicking William's dog, Jumble, in the village street. Technically, of course, he had some justification, because Jumble made what appeared to be an entirely unprovoked attack on him, barking furiously and pretending to bite his plus-fours. In reality, it was not unprovoked. They were very loud plus-fours, and Jumble, although generally of the meekest and mildest disposition possible, could not endure loud plus-fours. He always barked at them and pretended to bite them. They roused him to fury. Jumble perhaps looked upon himself as the sartorial censor of the village. Anyway, on the day on which Clarence appeared in a pair of green and mauve plus-fours (very green and very mauve) with red tabs, Jumble, after one glance at them, made his usual feint of attacking them, barking in shrill disapprobation till Clarence's foot sent him flying into the ditch.

The Outlaws met to consider what reprisals should be taken to avenge this insult to William's dog. It was William, curiously enough, who minimised the whole affair.

"Well," he said, "I don't *like* him, but—but I guess we'd better let him alone. You see, Jumble did bark at his trousers, an'—well, anyway, I guess we'd better let him alone."

The Outlaws were disappointed. William's attitude was felt to be unworthy of a leader with a reputation for avenging to the full any insult offered to him or his dog or to a member of his band. Ginger had a dark suspicion of the shameful truth. He had long been troubled by a secret suspicion that William admired Miss Holding —William, the leader, the scornful despiser of all women. The suspicion had depressed him very much.

The meeting broke up gloomily. William was aware that his prestige was dimmed, but he clung to his decision. Clarence, as guest and friend of Miss Holding, must not be harmed. Little did Clarence think, as he swaggered about the village with his receding chin and high-pitched laugh and general objectionableness, how narrowly he had been saved. Meeting William in the village he did not even recognise him as the master of the dog whom he had kicked into the ditch. And, not knowing how narrowly he had escaped retribution, he proceeded to rush on madly to his doom.

* * *

The Outlaws—William and Ginger and Douglas and Henry—were playing at Red Indians. They were playing at Red Indians in one of Farmer Jenks' fields. They were doing this because to play the game in Farmer Jenks' field lent it a certain excitement which it would otherwise have lacked.

Farmer Jenks hated the Outlaws with that bitter hatred which the landowner always bears to the habitual trespasser, and pursued them determinedly but unavailingly, whenever he caught sight of them. Therefore, Farmer Jenks, all unknown to himself, took an important part in the game. He represented a hostile tribe of especially ferocious redskins. However much the normal activities of the Red Indians as enacted by the Outlaws should pall, there was always the stimulating knowledge that at any minute the hostile tribe, as enacted by Farmer Jenks, might appear upon the scene, and this knowledge gave to the whole affair the spice of danger and excitement without which the Outlaws found life so barren. The game this afternoon was proceeding rather flatly.

A chestnut tree represented a tent. The Indians Eagle Eye, Red Hand, Lion Heart and Swiftfoot (otherwise William, Ginger, Douglas and Henry) were engaged in various pursuits. Eagle Eye was out killing wild animals for supper, Red Hand was climbing a tree so as to be on the look-out for enemies, Lion Heart was examining the "spoor" near the tent, and had just announced the recent passage of a herd of elephants and of hundreds of lions and tigers. Swiftfoot had gone out to collect twigs for a fire, but had soon tired of the pastime and was practising cart wheels by himself in a corner of the field.

Suddenly from Ginger's vantage ground came the shrill cry, "The Black Hearts," and the stout purple-faced form of Farmer Jenks was seen bearing down upon them in the distance, while Ginger himself was seen to shin down the tree trunk with almost incredible rapidity.

At once Eagle Eye leapt from his slaughter of wild animals, Lion Heart from his examinations of "spoor," and Swiftfoot from his cart wheels, and they set off across the field in headlong flight, two in either direction. They always split up into parties when fleeing from Farmer Jenks.

Farmer Jenks, of course, could not bear the thought that any of his quarry should elude him, and those fatal few moments during which he stood in the middle wondering which to follow, generally just enabled the Outlaws to escape. They would have escaped this time, too, if it hadn't been for Clarence.

Farmer Jenks stood hesitating as usual for those few fatal seconds in the middle of the field, then decided to pursue Douglas and Henry, who (despite Henry's tribal name) were slightly less fleet of foot than William and Ginger. And as I have said he would not have caught them if it hadn't been for Clarence.

Clarence happened to be passing down the road at the moment and witnessed the rout of the braves by the Black Hearts. Clarence was highly amused by the spectacle and decided to play a little joke on them on his own account.

So he stood at the stile, which was their only means of exit, and caught them. He then handed over Douglas to the perspiring and purple-faced Farmer Jenks and held the wriggling Henry till Farmer Jenks had quite finished with Douglas. Then he handed him Henry. And all the while he stood by, laughing his high-pitched laugh.

Farmer Jenks was, as matter of fact, too breathless to do himself full justice in the chastisement of his captures, but he did the best he could and then went panting and grunting back to his desecrated territory. Clarence, still laughing his high-pitched laugh, walked down the road. Douglas and Henry slowly and painfully rejoined William and Ginger in the old barn which was their usual meeting-place.

"*Well!*" began Douglas, in a tone of great bitterness and anguish.

"Yes," said William grimly, "we saw. We jolly well *saw*."

"Comes of lettin' him off when he kicked Jumble," went on Henry gloomily.

The silence that followed showed that the Outlaws considered this last outrage to be due solely to William's unwarrantable clemency on the former occasion. It was clear that even William himself felt guilty.

"Well," he said sternly, "we jolly well won't let him off *this* time."

"What'll we do to him?" said Henry as he sat down uneasily. (Douglas more widely did not attempt sitting down.) "I'd like to push him off a high precipice into the sea."

"Well, you can't," said Douglas the literal, "because there aren't any precipices here an' there isn't any sea. I'd like to kill him, shootin' arrows into him, same as they did Saint Someone or other in a picture."

"Well, that's silly," said William impatiently, "you'd

only get hung for murd'rin' him. Besides, *you* can't do *anything!* He saw you an' he'd know you by now. You leave this to me an' Ginger. We'll avenge you all right. Don't you worry. We'll jolly well avenge you. But you leave it all to us, 'cause he knows you, an' he don't know us. We were too far off for him to see us prop'ly."

"What'll you do?" said Douglas in the tone of one who thirsts for blood.

But William was a good tactician, forming no plans till he had surveyed the enemy's territory.

"We've gotter look round a bit first," he said. "You jus' leave it all to Ginger an' me."

* * *

Little did the smiling Clarence think, as he sat with his beloved by the river bank, that two boys were concealed in the bushes just behind him listening to his conversation. He had, of course, no eyes or ears for any but the beloved and he was finding it quite up-hill work because, although he'd been paying her attention now for nearly a fortnight, she didn't seem impressed or responsive.

She seemed, on the contrary, frankly bored, yawned frequently, and quite often forgot even to pretend that she was listening to him.

Clarence, who had a very good opinion of himself, thought that she was merely shy and diffident, and she was, of course, frightfully pretty.

So, unmoved by her silence and inadequate responses, he continued to address his attentions to her.

"May I take you for a drive to-morrow?" he pleaded.

"No," said Miss Holding very firmly. "I shan't be at home to-morrow. I'm going to some friends at Beechtop. I'm going to have lunch with them. Then we're going to take out our tea to the river bank and picnic there."

"May I come and help?" said Clarence.

"How could you help?" said Miss Holding brusquely.

"I could—er—wash up and carry things, and—er—bring you home."

She relented.

"All right. You can come over for tea if you like."

"Where shall I come—and when?" said Clarence.

"Come about four then," said Miss Holding, "to the bank near the church. It's rather pretty there. It's by the roadside, but there's a good stretch of bank with nice trees."

"I'll come," said Clarence fervently.

Then they got up and began to walk along the road to the village. Clarence's high-pitched laugh rang out as they went.

William and Ginger emerged from their leafy shelter and looked after the departing figures.

"I bet he's telling her about it," said Ginger gloomily.

"Well, what we've gotter do," said William, "is to go to this ole picnic an' see if we can't do somethin' to him there. I don't care if we *do* spoil her picnic."

He spoke rather wistfully. The sight and sound of Miss Holding had increased his admiration. But loyalty to her, of course, was as nothing to his loyalty to his Outlaws. Clarence had insulted Douglas and Henry and so Clarence must be punished. He hardened his heart against her.

"All right," said Ginger, and then mournfully, "but Beechtop's a *jolly* long way off. It's miles an' miles an' miles. How're we goin' to get there?"

"Walk," said William sternly.

Ginger groaned.

"We've *gotter* take a little trouble avengin' Douglas an' Henry," said William irritably. "We'll start early—d'rectly after lunch, an' we'll get there jus' about tea time, I bet."

* * *

They started directly after lunch and had they gone straight there they might easily have arrived before tea time. But the Outlaws, even when on vengeance bent, were still the Outlaws. They could not pass anything on a road which seemed to call for investigation. And the road positively teemed with such things. There was a pond which delayed them for quite a quarter of an hour. Then there was a tree which Ginger said William couldn't climb and which William therefore had to climb, though it took him ten minutes, and tore his coat and nearly broke his neck. Then there was a boy who jeered at William's personal appearance—both pond and tree had left their marks upon him—and was challenged by William to single combat. The fight lasted between five and ten minutes, then, battered but victorious, William rejoined Ginger and they resumed their journey.

"Wonder if we're nearly there," said Ginger.

"Course we aren't," said William, "it's ever so many miles yet."

"S'pose we don't get there before they've started home," said Ginger pessimistically.

"If you hadn't wasted all that time over that pond an' things——" said William, sublimely ignoring his own part in the delays.

"Well!" said Ginger indignantly, "well! I like that!—an' you climbin' trees an' fightin' boys an'—an' anyway, we don' even know what we're going' to do when we do get there."

"Somethin' sure to turn up to do when we get there," said William optimistically. "Trouble is," and his depression returned to him, "*gettin'* there—miles an' miles an' miles."

Just then they heard the sound of a motor cycle behind them and turned round.

"It's him," whispered William.

Clarence, be-goggled and wearing a radiant leather coat, flashed by. In flashing by he swerved slightly. Ginger sprang to one side, slipped and fell.

"Lie right down and keep your eyes shut," hissed William quickly.

Ginger obediently lay inert in the road.

"Hi!" called William after Clarence.

Clarence slowed down and turned round. He saw Ginger lying inert in the road and a look of horror came into his face. Slowly he wheeled his motor cycle back.

"I didn't knock him down," he said aggressively.

"Didn't you *just!*" said William severely. "You came right over this side of the road."

To his relief it was quite evident that Clarence did not recognise them. He had only seen them in the distance in Farmer Jenks' field. To him they were just two strange boys. Ginger still lay in the dust, his eyes closed.

Clarence took out his handkerchief and mopped his brow.

"I—er—I remember swerving a little. But I felt nothing. I'm sure I didn't go over him."

"No," said William rather regretfully, for it would be impossible even to pretend that any motor cycle had passed over the solid and obviously intact form of Ginger. "You didn't go *over* him, but you—you swerved right on to him an' gave him a t'riffic blow on his head. He's got—he's got," the word came with a flash of inspiration, " 'cussion. That's what he's got. He's got 'cussion."

"I don't believe he has," said Clarence, but he

sounded uncertain and he watched the motionless figure of Ginger anxiously.

"Well, he's unconscious, isn't he?" said William, in the tone of one who states an indubitable fact.

"I expect it just gave him a fright," said Clarence, then brightening, "anyway he looks healthy enough, doesn't he?"

"They always look healthy with 'cussion," said William darkly, and with such an air of knowledge that Clarence's face fell again. "I—I once knew a boy what had 'cussion jus' like that. A motor cycle swerved into him and he lay for a few minutes lookin' healthy—lookin' *very* healthy—that's one of the signs of 'cussion—unconscious jus' like that—an' soon he came round an' sat up an' said, 'Where am I?'—same as they always say—an' then he said that he'd got a most awful pain jus' above his ears—that's where you always feel the pain in 'cussion—an' they took him home moanin' an' groanin' somethin' t'riffic, an' lookin' quite healthy all the time same as they always do in 'cussion, an' he died jus' when he'd been at home for about an' hour, moanin' and groanin' somethin' t'riffic, he died. The man what swerved into him was put in prison."

"Nonsense!" said Clarence heartily, but he didn't look hearty and he didn't feel hearty.

William wore his most guileless expression. No one could look more like a boy who is telling the truth than William when he wasn't telling the truth. Experts had often been deceived by it. Just as Clarence stood trying to feel as hearty as he sounded and to rid himself of the effect of William's earnest words and guileless look, Ginger, in obedience to a surreptitious prod from William's foot, sat up in the dust and said, "Where am I?"

William bent over him in tender solicitude.

"You're here, Ginger dear, on the road." Then quite politely he effected the introduction. "This is the gentleman who knocked you down with his motor cycle."

Clarence blinked again, and again tried to be hearty.

"I'm quite sure you feel all right, my boy, now," he said.

But Ginger began to moan in a particularly resonant manner, rather like the mooing of a cow.

"Where do you feel the pain, Ginger dear?" inquired William tenderly.

Ginger stopped moaning to say:

"Jus' above my ears."

"*There!*" said William, as if greatly impressed. "It *is* 'cussion; I *said* it was 'cussion. Do you feel as if you could walk, Ginger dear?"

Ginger, who had started mooing again, stopped to say "No."

Clarence, who was beginning to look like a man in the grip of a nightmare, said:

"Where does he live?"

"At Beechtop," said William shamelessly, "jus' near the river."

"I—I'll take him home then," said the bewildered and apprehensive Clarence.

"Yes," said William. "I think we'd better get him home. Sometimes they go off so quick with 'cussion."

Between them they lifted the loudly moaning Ginger on to the pillion.

"I'll get on with him, shall I?" said William, "then if he goes off sudd'nly on the way, I can catch him."

William and Ginger enjoyed the drive to Beechtop tremendously. It was far nicer than walking. Ginger enjoyed it so much that he kept forgetting to moan and had to be recalled to his duty by kicks and prods from William. At Beechtop Clarence stopped.

"Where does he live exactly?" he inquired.

"Oh, it's jus' near here," said William. "Do you feel a little better, Ginger dear? Do you feel you could walk?"

"Yes," said Ginger, who had now stopped moaning, "I feel I could walk a bit now."

Clarence looked relieved and recovered something of his aplomb.

"Your own fault entirely," he said, "for not keeping right at the side of the road."

Then he went on to the river bank where Miss Holding and her friends awaited him.

He had completely forgotten the episode a few minutes later when he sat among the other guests on the bank, making little jokes and laughing his high-pitched laugh and handing round bags of cakes.

It was some time before he noticed William's face peering at him through the bushes making contortions which were obviously meant to be signs of some sort. The memory came back to him like the memory of a nightmare. His smile died away and his high-pitched laugh stopped abruptly on its highest note.

"I'll—er—I'll fetch some more cakes," he said, and went over to the provision basket near which William's face had loomed through the bushes.

Pretending to busy himself with the provisions, he snapped:

"Well?"

From behind the bushes where William's face had now discreetly withdrawn itself came a hoarse whisper:

"It is 'cussion. He's vi'lently ill."

"Well, I can't help it," hissed Clarence irritably. "He must have been standing right in the way. I can't do anything."

"No," said William. "No, I know you can't. But they

say he's gotter have a lot of nourishment an' his mother's not got any food in the house 'cause of them bein' very poor—*ever* so poor. So if you could let me have a few cakes an' things for him I'd take them to his house for him. The doctor says he can have rich things—he'd like some of those cakes with cream on——"

"All right," hissed Clarence. "I'll—I'll get some for you. Only—go away."

"If you sit down here an' put them behind you—I'll take 'em from you."

"All right," hissed Clarence, in a fever lest anyone should notice his visitor or hear his visitor's penetrating whisper. He sat down by the basket, very much irritated because it was right away from Miss Holding, and began to talk to a girl with red hair. As he talked he pushed cakes into the bushes. He talked excitedly and increasingly to divert attention from his activities and frequently stopped to mop his brow with his mauve silk handkerchief. He'd had a lot of nightmares in his life, but none as bad as this.

Meanwhile behind him in the bushes William and Ginger sat down happily to their splendid feast.

"It's most peculiar," Miss Holding was heard to say, "I can't think what's happened to all the iced cakes. We bought heaps, but they all seem to have gone."

"Most mysterious," said the girl with the red hair. "Never mind, we'll make the most of the biscuits."

Clarence began to talk to the red-haired girl again. He was just forgetting his fears and beginning to talk more or less sensibly when he felt a prod in the back.

"He's finished all those things what you sent," hissed William's voice, "an' the doctor says he's gotter have some more nourishment. His 'cussion's getting worse an' worse."

"I don't wonder if he's eaten all that stuff I gave you," said Clarence bitterly.

"You've gotter eat with 'cussion. It's the only thing to do to save your life—to go on eatin' an' eatin'. Can I have that bag of biscuits for him?"

"No."

"Well—I'll ask Miss Holding. P'r'aps if I tell her about you knockin' him down, she'll give me some for him." Hastily Clarence seized the bag of biscuits and pushed them into the bushes.

"Good heavens," said Miss Holding, looking around her a few minutes later, "all the biscuits seem to have gone now."

"It's always from Mr. Bergson's corner that things go," said the youngest guest, aged thirteen. "I've seen all the things just near him and then when you look again a minute later they aren't there."

Everyone turned and stared at Clarence who grew red to the tips of his ears.

"Well," he said at last desperately, "I—I've had quite a long drive. It—it makes one hungry."

"He must have eaten all that pound of biscuits as well as the two dozen iced cakes," said the youngest guest dispassionately.

"Hush dear," said her mother, reproachfully, and conversation became general, but Clarence could not help noticing that there seemed to be a tendency to avoid him. And things had hardly become normal again when he felt once more that painful prod in the back that heralded William's penetrating whisper:

"I've just been to see him again and——"

"I'm not giving you anything else," hissed Clarence.

"No. He doesn't want anything now. He's too ill to eat now. His 'cussion's something t'riffic now. They're awful mad about it. His father's just sent for a policeman——"

CLARENCE TALKED EXCITEDLY TO DIVERT ATTENTION, AND AS HE TALKED HE PUSHED CAKES INTO THE BUSHES.

"*What?*"

"To take down all about you knockin' 'im down, case he dies and you have to go to prison."

The red-haired girl turned to Clarence.

"Were you speaking to me, Mr. Bergson?" she said politely.

Clarence took out his mauve silk handkerchief and mopped his brow again.

"Y-yes," he said, "I was just remarking what—er-—what a beautiful view."

"Do you think so?" said the red-haired girl coldly (she simply couldn't get over this man's having eaten two dozen iced cakes and a pound of biscuits). "I think it's very ordinary."

William and Ginger had left the bushes. Gorged with cakes and in a state of hazy content they were walking

"IT'S MOST PECULIAR," SAID MISS HOLDING. "I CAN'T THINK WHAT'S HAPPENED TO ALL THE ICED CAKES."

down the road towards a point at the road where a policeman stood directing the very scanty traffic which came from a side road. They had not finished with Clarence yet. The Outlaws never went in for half measures. On the way they passed a public house called "The Staff of Life," and on a bench just outside lounged an enormous man with cross-eyes and abnormally long arms and wearing a smile which in the distance looked ferocious, but on nearer approach became merely fatuous. William and Ginger watched him with interest as they passed him and then, forgetting him, approached the policeman.

William assumed his expression of innocence.

"Please sir," he said, "there's a gentleman down there what's just had his pocket picked. He told me to go'n see if I could find a policeman."

The policeman took out a pocket-book.

"Who is he?" he said eagerly. Evidently he welcomed the interruption. There had only been one cart along the side road in the last three-quarters of an hour.

"He's with a picnic party down by the bank," said William guilelessly, "he's dressed in a leather coat."

Then William and Ginger melted silently away. The policeman, still holding his note-book, went down to the bank.

Clarence was just beginning to feel that he was returning to favour. He was talking about his motor-cycle.

"Sixty miles an hour is nothing to me," he said, "there's no danger at all to a good driver in sixty miles an hour."

"That's what makes you so hungry, I suppose," said the youngest guest, as if a problem which had long been troubling her were solved at last.

Her mother said, "Hush, dear," and again the atmosphere was slightly strained.

"How fast did you come here to-day, Mr. Bergson?" said the youngest guest's mother, feeling that it was up to her to restore the atmosphere.

Clarence's complacency dropped from him as he thought of how fast he'd come there.

"Oh—er—it varied," he said absently.

What had that little wretch said? A policeman taking down details! It was a horrible thought. He took out the mauve silk handkerchief and wiped his brow again. His mauve silk handkerchief was becoming quite damp. And then—his eyes almost started out of his head. Here

ALL ALONG BY THE RIVER BANK WENT CLARENCE, AND BEHIND HIM IN HOT PURSUIT CAME THE POLICEMAN.

was the policeman coming down the river bank and right up to him—the policeman who must have come straight from the bedside of the boy he'd knocked down—with his note-book in his hand.

Clarence didn't stop to think. He leapt to his feet and took to his heels. The policeman didn't stop to think either. He saw someone running away from him so, from sheer force of habit, he ran after him. Along the road by the river bank went Clarence, and behind him in hot pursuit, the stalwart figure of the policeman.

"Well!" said the picnic party, giving inadequate expression to its feelings.

"He seemed to me all afternoon," said the girl with red hair, darkly, "like a man with something on his mind."

"Fancy him being able to run like that," said the youngest guest admiringly, "when he's just eaten two dozen iced cakes and a pound of biscuits. I couldn't."

"Hush, dear," said her mother absently.

"There was something about a murder in this morning's paper," said the girl with red hair. "I shouldn't be a bit surprised if he did it."

"Surely not," objected someone.

"Well, why should a policeman come for him and he run off like this? Most of these murders in the papers are done by quite ordinary people living quite ordinary lives, you know. He must be one of them. I expect he'll have caught him by now. He'll be hung of course."

"Well, he'll have had a jolly good tuck-in first," said the youngest guest.

"Hush, dear," said her mother. "Of course it may not be an actual murder. It may be merely robbing a bank or forging a will or something."

"I've always wanted to know a criminal," said the girl with red hair, heaving a sigh of content, "and I've thought he seemed queer all the afternoon. He's been muttering to himself into the bushes and behaving most peculiarly all the time."

"Well, if you don't mind," said the youngest guest's mother, "I'll take girlie home. One doesn't want to be mixed up in this sort of thing—as a witness or jury or anything—and one never knows who a murderer will murder next. They say that it sort of grows on them. If he's overpowered the policeman—and criminals have the strength of ten men—or is that lunatics?—he may be coming back here in search of fresh victims. He's probably got homicidal mania

—breaking out in spasms, you know."

She collected the youngest guest and drifted away.

"I think I'll go too," said the girl with red hair. "I don't believe in running unnecessary risks and one does hear of such things in the papers. I could tell the minute I set eyes on him that he wasn't normal."

Gradually the other guests followed her example, and when Clarence finally returned panting and breathless, only Miss Holding was left by the river bank among the ruins of the feast. Or rather only Miss Holding was apparently left, for William and Ginger had returned to their leafy shelter and were watching with interest to see what turn events would take.

"Well!" said Miss Holding, as Clarence, holding on to his sides with both hands, came panting up to her and sank on the river bank by her side. "What in the world——?

"A mistake," gasped Clarence, "he'd heard—that a man—had had his—pocket picked—thought it—was me—mistake."

"But why on earth did you run away?" said Miss Holding.

"I—I don't know," panted Clarence.

"I remember once reading about a man who did that," said Miss Holding. "He'd had an awful dream about a policeman coming for him and the next day he took to his heels as soon as he set eyes on one."

"Yes," said Clarence, eagerly accepting the explanation, "that was what happened to me. I had a most terrible dream about a policeman last night and as soon as I saw this one coming up to me my—my dream sort of—came over me again and I—I just ran away. Force of association!"

Miss Holding laughed.

"Well. I think I can squeeze you out another cup of

tea to refresh you and there's a lot of plain cake left in spite of the mysterious disappearance of the iced ones."

* * *

Clarence lay back on the river bank and smoked cigarettes and drank tea and ate plain cake. Then, refreshed and invigorated, he began to talk again. He began to talk about himself.

He began to tell her all about his past life—what noble and heroic things he had done and what a noble and heroic character he was. Miss Holding was kind to him. She led him on. The listeners' spirits fell. This was not how they had meant their vengeance to end—in this pleasant conversation on the river bank. All they seemed to have done was to have cleared the stage for Clarence's courtship.

And it was quite evident that Clarence had completely forgotten his victim who now lay (presumably) in the throes of concussion. They were full of virtuous horror at the thought. Then they turned and looked at each other—Ginger with the serene, trusting face of one who knows that his leader will evolve some plan, and William with that ferocious scowl which in William betokened deep thought. Then suddenly the scowl cleared and there flashed across his freckled face the light that betokened inspiration.

"I'll just go down to the river and wash this cup," Miss Holding was saying. "No, don't move. As a matter of fact I'd much rather wash it myself. I never let anyone else wash my picnic cups. They don't do them properly."

Clarence, nothing loth, remained on the bank in the sunshine while Miss Holding went down to the water. Then—just as Clarence's thoughts were happily flitting round the attractive figure that he imagined himself to be cutting—suddenly that awful boy's face appeared through the bushes again making horrible grimaces. The smile dropped from Clarence's face.

"Go away!" he hissed, putting out a hand to push William's face back into the bushes.

"I've just come from him," said William. "He's ever so much worse."

"It's not my fault," hissed Clarence.

"I know it isn't," said William sympathetically. "I keep tellin' 'em it wasn't really your fault an' that you didn't run over him on purpose, but they won't listen to me. His father's out lookin' for you now. He's an awful man with cross-eyes an' very long arms. He says he's going to wring your neck."

Clarence went pale, but at that moment Miss Holding returned from washing up the cup, and Clarence, relieved at the sudden disappearance of William's face, made an effort to entertain her again. He told her about the time he had made a century at cricket at his prep. school, but somehow, despite the fact that she was obviously impressed, he couldn't put any real zest into the narrative. Cross-eyed and with very long arms.

Meanwhile William and Ginger were creeping silently away from the bushes. It was not for nothing that the Outlaws played Red Indians nearly every day. Not even the cracking of a twig betrayed their passage.

Outside on the main road they looked cautiously up and down to see if the policeman (who was presumably thirsting for their blood) was anywhere in sight. To their relief he wasn't, and to their still greater relief the cross-eyed man was. He was still sitting on the seat outside "The Staff of Life," contemplating the road crossways with his ferocious smile. William assumed his guileless expression again and they approached him.

"Please, sir," began William politely, "would you like a few cakes?"

The man glared at him and at Ginger simultaneously, and smiled his ferocious smile.

"Wouldn't mind," he admitted, condescendingly.

"Well," went on William, "there's a gentleman an' a lady havin' a picnic down on the river bank jus' behind those bushes, an' the gentleman told me to find someone what'd like the cakes what's left over an' send 'em to him to fetch 'em."

The man rose slowly.

"Well—I don't mind," he said, and set off towards the river bank.

Clarence had passed on from the story of the century he had made at his prep. school and was telling her about the time when he'd put a drawing-pin on a master's chair at his public school.

Miss Holding seemed very much interested. Everything seemed to be going very nicely. His spirits were gradually rising. He didn't believe that he'd really hurt the boy or that his father was out looking for him. "Cross-eyed and long arms"—it was ridiculous. He wouldn't be surprised if that wretched boy had made up the whole thing.

Then suddenly he stopped short. His eyes bulged and his mouth dropped open. A man with cross-eyes and long arms and a ferocious smile was coming down the river bank, towards him. It was true. It was the boy's father coming to wring his neck.

With a yell of terror as loud and shrill as a factory siren Clarence leapt to his feet, leapt over the bushes and rushed down the road. He did not stop running till he reached home.

The cross-eyed man and Miss Holding stood gazing after his retreating figure. Then the cross-eyed man turned, and looking simultaneously at Miss Holding and the bushes said with dispassionate interest:

"IT'S A PITY WE GAVE HIM ALL THE BUNS," SAID MISS HOLDING, "BECAUSE I'M SURE YOU WOULD HAVE LIKED SOME."

" 'As somethin' stung him?"

"I don't know *what's* happened to him," said Miss Holding.

"Well," said the cross-eyed man, abandoning all attempts to solve the mystery of Clarence's flight, "they told me that if I came along 'ere they'd give me some cake."

"You can have all that's left," said Miss Holding, "but who told you?"

One of the cross-eyed man's eyes had espied a movement in the neighbouring bushes. He dived into it and emerged holding William by his collar.

"This 'ere nipper," he said.

* * *

The cross-eyed man had departed with his booty.

William and Ginger sat on the river bank on either side of Miss Holding.

"It's a pity we gave him all the buns and plain cake," said Miss Holding, "because I'm sure you'd have liked some."

"No, thanks," said William politely, and added with perfect truth, "we—we've sort of had enough."

A gleam of intelligence shone in Miss Holding's eyes.

"How long have you been in that bush?" she said.

"Quite a long time," said William, "on and off."

"Perhaps," said Miss Holding, "you accounted for the two dozen iced cakes and the pound of biscuits."

William assumed his guileless expression.

"Well," he admitted, "Mr. Bergson did kin'ly give us something to eat."

"Suppose," said Miss Holding, "that you tell me all about it." So they told her.

At the end she dried her eyes and said: "It's perfectly

priceless and the best part of it all is that I'm sure it will make him go home."

And it did.

They had a lovely journey home packed into Miss Holding's two-seater, and the first person they saw in the village was Mrs. Holding.

"Whatever's happened to Clarence?" said Mrs. Holding.

"What has?" said Miss Holding.

"He came home in a most peculiar condition," went on Mrs. Holding. "He said he'd been running all the way. And he took the first train back to town and wants his things sent on after him. He told me not to give his address to anyone."

"I'm *so* glad," said Miss Holding serenely, "because I was getting bored even with pulling his leg."

"But what happened?" said her mother.

"He just got up and ran home, didn't he, children?" said Miss Holding dreamily. "I should think that he suffers from spasmodic insanity. These two little boys have been such a help to me this afternoon, mother. Come and let's find somewhere to have an ice cream, children."

William hesitated.

"We oughter g'n' tell Douglas and Henry that we've avenged them first," he said.

"Good," said Miss Holding. "Go and find them and bring them along too, and we'll all go and have ices somewhere."

And as William remarked blissfully that evening, it was one of the jolliest vengeances they'd ever had.

Chapter 6

Parrots for Ethel

The Outlaws were depressed. Ordinary pursuits had lost their charms. They neither ran nor leapt nor played Red Indians nor ranged the countryside nor carried on guerrilla warfare with the neighbouring farmers. Instead they held meetings in each other's back gardens, in each other's shrubberies and summer-houses and tool-sheds, eloquently discoursing on the gravity of the situation, but finding no remedy for it.

The cause of the whole trouble was the fatal attractiveness of William's sister Ethel. Not that William or any of his friends actually admitted the fatal attractiveness. Ethel was to them an ordinary disagreeable "grown up" with a haughty manner and impossible standards of cleanliness, who happened also to possess a combination of red hair and blue eyes that had a strange and unaccountable effect upon adult members of the opposite sex. They cherished always a stern and bitter contempt for Ethel's admirers. And now Douglas's brother George and Ginger's brother Hector had joined the number. It is impossible to describe the shame and horror the Outlaws felt at this. That any member of any family of theirs should stoop to the supreme indignity of admiring Ethel. . . . William felt as deeply outraged as any of them. He felt that the infatuation of Douglas's brother and Ginger's brother for his sister exposed the whole body of Outlaws to the scorn of their friends and the laughter of their foes.

The possibility of it had hitherto never even occurred to them. Douglas's brother George and Ginger's brother Hector, though objectionable in every other way as only elder brothers can be, had at least been satisfactory in that, almost as much as the Outlaws themselves, they held the female sex in scorn. It was Ethel's influenza that seemed to have made the difference. Ethel had withdrawn from public life for a term of fourteen days or so with the high temperature, the streaming eyes and the settled pessimism which, taken together, constitute Influenza. Evidently the sudden absence of Ethel's familiar figure from the lanes and roads of her native village awoke strange feelings in the breast of George and Hector, and the emergence of Ethel from her sick room at the end of the fortnight with, as it seemed by contrast with her absence, redoubled beauty, completed their enslavement. They abandoned their old manner of cold indifference to her. They smiled at her ingratiatingly, they bought new ties and new socks, they waited at spots that it was probable that Ethel would pass. Their old friendship with each other cooled. When waiting at the same spot for a word or a glance from Ethel they affected not to see each other. They passed each other in the village street with no other recognition than a scornful curl of the lip. They no longer discussed the football results with each other. In the privacy of their home circle they naturally vented all the bitterness of the pangs of love upon their younger brothers.

* * *

The Outlaws had met in the summer-house of William's garden. Henry was away staying with an aunt and only the three deeply involved parties—William, Douglas and Ginger—were present.

"People *laughin'* at 'em," said Douglas bitterly. "I know they are from somethin' someone said to me yesterday. S'nice for *me*," he added with an air of impersonal bitterness, "s'nice for *me* havin' a brother what everyone's laughin' at."

"'S jus' as bad for me," retorted Ginger. "An' 's not only that. It's makin' Hector crabbier an' crabbier at home."

This reminded Douglas of his latest grievance.

"Took it off me," he said fiercely, "took it off me and threw it away. An' it was new too. 'S no good at all now. Threw it into the ditch an' it's full of mud now an' won't play anyway whatever I do. It's ru'ned. An' it was the best mouth-organ I've ever had. It made a noise you could hear for miles and miles. And he took it off me 'n' threw it away. An' I wasn't makin' much noise. I was only practisin'—practisin' jus' outside his room. Well, *I* din' know he was makin' up po'try about Ethel. He needn't 've come out roarin' mad at me like that. I bet I've got 's much right to practise my mouth-organ as he's got writin' po'try to Ethel."

"Jus' *'xactly* what Hector did to me 'n my trumpet last night," said Ginger, torn between impersonal interest in the coincidence and a personal sense of grievance at the memory of his wrongs. "Came out ravin' mad at me jus' 'cause I was sittin' on the top of the stairs practisin' a trumpet. Came ravin' mad out of his room an' took it off me an' broke it. *D'lib'rately* broke it. I bet *he* he was writin' po'try 'bout Ethel too." He threw William a cold glance. "Seems to me," he said, "a pity some people can't stop their sisters going' about the world makin' all this mis'ry. Breakin' people's trumpets an' throwin' people's mouth-organs away."

"*Ethel* din't break your trumpets an' throw your mouth-organs away," said William with spirit. "Pity some people can't stop their brothers actin' so stupid whenever they see a girl."

"They don't," retorted Ginger, "they've never done it before. They've always acted to girls same as we do—till this set-out with Ethel," he ended gloomily.

"Well," said William with odious complacency, "that only proves that Ethel's nicer 'n all the other girls."

Their attitude seemed to be inexplicably deteriorating from a common, lofty scorn of the work of the blind god to a partisanship each of his particular family.

"Oh, it does, does it?" said Ginger aggressively.

But William was not to be drawn into personal combat on behalf of Ethel. He was, as a matter of fact, a little bored with the whole proceedings. He disapproved of the situation no less than he had always disapproved of it, but meeting in summer-houses and tool-sheds and discoursing on it did not seem to make it any better and meanwhile the days of the holidays were slipping by wasted. Moreover, the day before an uncle of William's had taken him up to London, and so William was taking for the time being a broader perspective of life than his friends.

"Never mind," he said pacifically. "There's other things to do than keep talkin' about it an' there's other people in the world 'sides Ethel an' your ole George an' Hector."

"Yes," said Douglas bitterly, "you'd say that if it was *your* mouth-organ, wun't you?"

"An' you'd say that if it was *your* trumpet," said Ginger. "Huh! I bet I've not got other things to do than forget about that trumpet."

"Come to that," said William, "Ethel took my bow an' arrer off me yesterday 'cause it accident'ly came through her window and broke an ole vase, but I don' keep talkin' about it."

But Ginger refused to be drawn from his grievance.

"He oughter be made to give me a new one," he said, and added with a melancholy sigh, "An' jus' to think that wherever there's grown-up brothers there's things like this hap'nin' all over the country what never get into the newspaper an' England supposed to be a free country—people's trumpets bein' took off them an' *broke* for no reason at all. What's that if it's not tyranny what the history books talk about? All I c'n say is," he added darkly, "that all those Magna Charter an' things what the history books say brought Lib'ty to England don' seem to've done *me* much good."

But Douglas had at last, like William, tired of the subject.

"What did your uncle take you to see yesterday, William?" he said.

"He took me to a place with a lot of dead animals—stuffed mostly—but some skeletons—an' a man givin' lectures on 'em—tellin' us about them an' what they were like an' what they did."

"Was he int'restin'?" said Ginger temporarily relinquishing his grievance, as no one would listen to it any longer.

"Yes," said William simply, "he'd got a loose tooth what you could see movin' when he talked, an' there was a boy there what thought he could make faces better'n me, but he found out in the end he jolly well couldn't."

The atmosphere was certainly lightened by this breath from the outside world. The Outlaws began to think that perhaps they had discussed the Ethel-George-Hector affair to satiety and the description of William's excursion of yesterday might afford a little more interest.

"Did he give you a nice dinner, William?" said Douglas.

"Crumbs, yes!" said William, "he let me choose what I'd have for dinner an' I had six ices an' then there were some things like cakes with heaps 'n' heaps of cream on an' I had twelve of them an' then I had a bottle of orange squash an' then I had two plates of trifle."

"No meat nor potatoes?" said Ginger.

"No," said William, and added in simple explanation, "I c'n get meat an' potatoes at home."

There was a silence during which the Outlaws wistfully contemplated the mental vision of William's dinner. Then Ginger said bitterly: "That's the best of uncles. You'd never catch an aunt letting you have a dinner like that," and he added plaintively, "all mine seem to be aunts."

"What sort of animals were they, William?" asked Douglas.

"All sorts," said William, "an'"—slowly—"I've been thinkin'. It'd be quite easy to get up a show like that but with live animals 'stead of stuffed ones. I know," he said quickly, forestalling possible objection, "that we've often tried shows *somethin'* like that but not *quite* like. We've never tried lecturin' on 'em. We've tried havin' 'em for a circus and we've tried sellin' 'em but we've never tried *lecturin'* on 'em."

"Well, who can lecture on 'em?" said Douglas.

"I can," said William promptly. "I heard that man doin' it an' so I bet I know how to do it now."

"Can you woggle your teeth?" said Douglas

"It's not *ne'ssary* to woggle your teeth lecturin' on animals," said William coldly. "'Sides, I bet I could if I wanted to."

"I could bring my dormouse," said Ginger.

"An' there's my insecks," said William, "an' Jumble an'—all our cats."

"That's not *much*," said Douglas. "How do they get animals for the big places like the Zoo?"

"People lend 'em," said Ginger, "or give 'em. I've often heard of people givin' 'em. When the Roy'l Fam'ly goes abroad for its holiday people give 'em animals an' they bring 'em home and give 'em to the Zoo."

"Seems a funny sort of thing to do," said Douglas incredulously.

"Well, I've read about it in newspapers so it mus' be true."

" 'F what my father says about newspapers is true," objected Ginger, "nothin' in any of 'em's true."

"*Somethin'* in *some* of 'em *must* be," objected Douglas, "'cause——"

William determinedly dragged the conversation back from the possible truth or untruth of newspapers to the matter in hand.

"Well, 'bout these animals," he said. "We'll have it in our summer-house an' I'll lecture on 'em an' we'll have all our cats an' Jumble an' we'll c'leck some more insecks an' we'll have Ginger's dormouse an' we'll get people to lend us other animals or p'raps give us 'em."

"Who?" said Douglas gloomily.

"Who what?"

"Who you think'll give us *anythin'*, much less an animal."

"Oh, do shut up," said William irritably, "carryin' on jus' as if nothin' ever turned out right."

"Well, nothin' ever does," said Douglas, hotly defending his pessimism. "Look at the time you——"

"Oh, both of you shut up," said Ginger, "an' let's go an' fetch the dormouse."

They passed the drawing-room where Ethel sat with George on one side of her and Hector on the other. To be quite frank Ethel was a minx who, while remaining always provokingly heart-whole, liked to have as many admirers as possible around her.

Silence and a certain depression fell on the group as the younger brothers of it passed the window.

"He drove me half mad with a beastly mouth-organ yesterday," groaned George, "till I took it from him and chucked it into the pond."

"Same here with a trumpet," said Hector, and added severely, "seems to me extraordinary what boys are like nowadays. I'm quite sure *we* were never like that."

"Well, I'm sure no boy ever anywhere was half as bad as William," said Ethel with a sigh. "He broke a vase that was one of my greatest treasures yesterday with his bow and arrow. He really *is* the worst of the lot."

Both Hector and George made an inarticulate murmur that might either have been half-hearted protest or deep sympathy, but neither of them seriously disputed the statement.

"Ginger's pretty bad, though," said Hector with a judicial air; "last week he had one of those awful things that are supposed to sound like a dog barking."

"William had a thing," said Ethel dreamily, "that was supposed to sound like a bird chirping only it didn't. It sounded like—well, I don't know what it sounded like, but it went through and *through* my head."

"What a *shame*," said Hector and George simultaneously in passionate indignation. Their tone implied that they were lusting for William's blood.

"After all," continued Ethel happily, burbling on in the serene consciousness that it didn't really matter what she said because every single word of it would be heavenly wisdom in the ears of the infatuated youths, "after all a bird's chirp is quite a nice soft sound. I'm very fond of birds."

"What sort do you like best?" said George and Hector simultaneously. They glared at each other suspiciously as they spoke. Each had decided to give Ethel a present of her favourite bird in as ornamental a cage as his means would allow on her next birthday, and each had a horrible suspicion that the other had the same project in mind.

"I think that parrots are rather sweet," said Ethel. "Don't you?"

Neither spoke, because neither did consider parrots rather sweet and both were having sudden misgivings about the price of parrots. . . . Didn't parrots cost an awful lot of money—a matter of pounds, unless, of course, one could meet a sailor just returned from foreign parts with one, and probably even he would demand its market price. A canary now . . . both had hoped she'd say a canary. Both had had pleasing visions of themselves presenting Ethel with a very yellow canary in a very ornate cage adorned with a very blue bow . . . the vision included Ethel's delight, her cries of rapture, her sudden realisation that nowhere else would she meet with such tenderness, such understanding, such undying devotion as in this hero who remembered even what sort of bird she liked best, who—anyway, it was all very romantic and there was a beautiful wedding and they lived happily ever after. When the canary was dead, of course, she had it stuffed and it was always one of her dearest treasures. But a parrot . . . no, one could never wax sentimental over a parrot. A parrot would never surely inaugurate a romance.

"You can teach it such jolly things to say," went on Ethel. "I remember once a friend of mine had to go into quarantine for measles or something like that and a friend of hers gave her a parrot to be company for her. He gave it her in rather a nice way, too. He put it on the garden seat on the lawn and sent in a letter to say that if she would look out of her window she would see a little friend who had come to keep her company. Or something like that. She was always devoted to that parrot."

Both George and Hector checked an impulse to ask whether she married him. Each would have asked it had the other not been present, but there are certain questions which are more effective when asked without an audience. George and Hector walked home together but in silence. The only thing they wanted to talk about was Ethel, but they didn't want to talk about Ethel to each other. Hector decided that if George won her he would go out to Africa to shoot big game. George, being of a less subtle nature, had decided that if Hector won her he would drown himself in the village pond. But neither was really uneasy because neither thought that the other would win her. After all, thought George, she hadn't looked at Hector in that meaning way she'd looked at him when she said good-bye, and, after all, thought Hector, she hadn't pressed George's hand as she'd pressed his on parting. . . .

They met the Outlaws on their way to William's house reverently carrying among them what was to be the star turn of the lecture, Ginger's dormouse.

The Outlaws and Ethel's suitors looked at each other coldly and without recognition as they passed, but really the Outlaws had the best of the encounter because they could turn round and make grimaces expressive of scorn and derision at the back of their foes, and because they knew that their foes had an uneasy suspicion that they were doing this but considered it inconsistent with their dignity to look back to make sure.

* * *

It was the next morning. Ethel was staring wildly at a letter she held in her hand.

"Daphne's got measles and I was with her last night. What shall I do?"

"You'll have to go into quarantine, I'm afraid, dear," said her mother placidly.

"My goodness!" said Ethel in a tone of horror and despair, and feeling the exclamation inadequate, changed it to "Great Heavens!"

After a pause indicative of deep feeling she continued: "Why, only yesterday I was telling George and Hector about the time Luxy Foxe had it and what's-his-name sent her a parrot. It seems as it just mentioning the thing had brought it on me. Well, I shall die of boredom, that's all. Do you mean to say that I've got to stay in the room *all* the time."

"Yes, dear," said her mother and added placidly, "there's quite a nice view."

Ethel went to the window. From it she could see Ginger, Douglas and William clustered round the dormouse's cage by the side of the lawn.

"*That's* a lovely view, isn't it?" she said bitterly.

William had received the news that Ethel would have to be in quarantine for measles without emotion or indeed without interest of any sort. He had no time or thought or sympathy to spare for Ethel. A more terrible tragedy had happened than Ethel's quarantine. The dormouse had died in the night. There was no sign to show how it had died. It was certainly not starvation. It had died in the midst of plenty. There were no marks of violence on the body. Douglas had a theory that some of the berries picked promiscuously in the garden for its nourishment yesterday by Ginger from any tree or bush that provided berries of any sort had not agreed with it. Ginger hotly contested this theory.

"That's what berries are *for*," he said indignantly. "That's what Nachur provides berries on trees for—to feed animals with."

William interrupted the discussion to suggest that as long as hygiene should allow, the dead body of the dormouse should be exhibited as a stuffed one. "No one'll know it isn't," he added hopefully, "not without cuttin' it open and we won't let 'em do that. We'll jus' say it's a stuffed dormouse an' I'll talk about it a bit, tellin' about its habits—sleepin' an' such like, an' p'r'aps it won't be so bad."

His optimism was unconvinced and unconvincing. He knew that no stuffed dormouse could compensate for the sight of Ginger's dormouse going round and round on its little wheel. They took the dead body to the summer-house, leaving William alone on the lawn gloomily considering the prospects of his lecture thus deprived of its star turn.

He did not at first see Ginger's brother Hector who had come round to the side of the house looking pale and distraught.

"This is terrible news," began Hector.

William was touched. Somehow he hadn't expected this kindness, this understanding, from Hector.

"Yes, isn't it," he acquiesced despondently, "terrible."

"She seemed all right yesterday," continued Hector.

"She was," affirmed William, "she was quite all right yesterday. I think it was eatin' those berries."

"What berries?" said the young man.

"Those berries Ginger gave her."

"D—did Ginger give her some berries?" stammered Hector aghast.

"Yes—all sorts of different coloured kinds of berries what he found about the garden. And she ate them all."

The horror of the young man is indescribable. That *his* young brother—*his* young brother should be the cause of it. . . .

"B-but," he stammered, "I—I heard in the village it was measles."

"No," said William, "it's worse than measles. She's dead. She died in the night."

"*What?*" screamed the young man.

"She's dead," said William, somewhat flattered if a little surprised by the deep emotion shown by the visitor. "When Ginger 'n' me came to clean out her cage this mornin' we found her dead."

"Clean out her c——! What the dickens are you talking about?"

"Our mouse," said William simply; "weren't you?"

The visitor obviously controlled himself with an effort.

"No," he said with venomous coldness, "I was talking about your sister Ethel."

"Oh, Ethel——" said William carelessly. "Oh no, it's not measles. It's somethin' else. I've forgotten its name."

Again anxiety clouded the young man's brow.

"N-nothing serious, I hope?" he said.

"Dunno," said William, "might be, I suppose. I simply can't understand it dyin' like that. I mean I've always thought that if berries were pois'nous, an'mals din' eat them. I always thought that an'mals had some special way of tellin' pois'nous stuff."

Again the young man restrained himself with difficulty from inflicting actual physical injury upon William.

"Is your sister allowed visitors?" he asked.

"Ethel?" said William as if bringing his mind with an effort from an affair of vital and universal importance to one of no significance at all. "No. She's got the sort of illness that she's not ill with, but she's not got to see people. It's got a name but I've forgot it. It looked all right last night. It ate Ginger's berries about six o'clock an' it looked all right when we left it. If you want to know what *I* think, I think that someone's poisoned it. I think——"

"You mean she's in quarantine?" interrupted Ginger's brother Hector.

"No," said William irritably, "I keep tellin' you—she's dead."

"Shut up about your beastly mouse," commanded Ginger's brother Hector fiercely. "I don't care two pins for your beastly mouse——"

"Oh, you don't, don't you?" muttered William darkly.

"No, I don't. It's your sister I'm talking about. You mean that she's in quarantine."

"Yes," said William, "that's the name of what she's got. Dun't seem to have made much difference to her 'cept makin' her temper a bit worse than usual and that's sayin' *somethin'*."

Hector turned on his heel contemptuously and strode away, his brow drawn into a thoughtful frown. He'd remembered suddenly what Ethel had said about the parrot. He'd get a parrot. He'd write a note such as she said her friend's friend had written about a little friend to keep her company, and leave the parrot in the garden as her friend's friend had done. She had seemed to think it was a beautiful thought. He'd do it . . . it would, he was sure, touch her deeply. If only that wretched fellow George didn't think of it too. He'd hurry home and do it quickly before George thought of it. He met George on the road, acknowledged him with distant hauteur and passed on his way.

William remained upon the garden bench plunged in

gloom. The death of the dormouse had imperilled all his plans. He felt that he could have lectured indefinitely upon the dormouse as it went round and round on its little wheel or even as it blinked at them or ate its food, but a stiff, dead dormouse even camouflaged as a "stuffed" exhibit was quite a different affair. It would, he was afraid, fall very flat indeed. But William was never the boy to own himself beaten. He was searching about in his mind for some other exhibit to take the place of the live dormouse when the shadow of George fell upon him and the voice of George broke upon his meditations.

"Well, I'm very sorry to hear this," began George.

William's heart warmed to him. Here, at any rate, was sympathy. . . .

"Yes," he said, "it was an awful shock to us all to find her dead this mornin'."

"*What?*" screamed George.

Explanation followed. It appeared that George also did not care two pins about the beastly mouse, and they parted coldly. George walked quickly down the road. He'd suddenly remembered what Ethel had said about the parrot yesterday. He'd get her one. . . . He'd give it her in the same way as she said that her friend's friend had given one to her. She'd seemed to think that there was something very graceful about it. It would please her. He'd hurry home now so as to do it before Hector thought of it. . . .

William rejoined the others in the summer-house.

"Takin' your mouth-organs an' trumpets off you," he said bitterly, "an' carin' more about someone bein' ill than someone *dyin*'. An' she's not even reely ill, either. If I get a chance," he added darkly. "I'll make 'em buy you *new* mouth-organs an' trumpets, an' make her give me back my bow an' arrer."

"Well, you aren't likely to get a chance," said the victims without much gratitude, "an' the thing to do now is to try'n find a few more animals for lecturin' on. A dead dormouse an' a few insecks isn't much."

William considered this a minute in silence, then he said:

"Tell you what. We'll put up a notice askin' people to lend us an'mals or give us an'mals like what they do to the Zoo."

this suggestion seemed to infuse new life into them. Their gloom departed.

"Who'll write it an' where'll we put it?" said Ginger.

"I'll write it," said William, "an' we'll put it on the side gate-post. Quite a lot of people go along the lane by the side gate. We'll put it up an' then we'll go out'n look for some more int'restin' insecks."

"If we all go out," objected Ginger, "there'll be no one to take the an'mals when they bring them."

The Outlaws tried to visualise a queue of people waiting by the side gate each in charge of a rare and interesting animal, but even to their optimism the vision lacked reality.

"Of course," admitted William, "it's jus' *possible* that no one'll see it—at least no one what's got an an'mal or at least no one what's got an an'mal what they want to lend us. It doesn't hardly seem worth while any of us stayin' behind jus' on the chance when we might be out catchin' int'restin' insecks."

"Let's put somethin' on the notice," suggested Ginger, "tellin' 'em to take 'em to the summer-house an' leave 'em there."

"Yes," said William sarcastically, "an' havin' 'em eatin' up or fightin' our insecks. You don' know what sort of wild creatures they may bring—all fightin' each other an' eatin' each other up in the summer-house.

'Sides, you can see the summer-house from the road an' we'll be gettin' 'em all stolen by thieves what see them as they pass. No, I vote we shut up the summer-house while we're away an' put somethin' on the notice tellin' 'em where to leave them. They can leave 'em somewhere where they can't be seen from the road." He pondered the problem in silence for a few seconds, frowning thoughtfully, then his face cleared. "I know . . . we'll tell 'em to put 'em on the seat in the back garden, 'cause no one can see that from the road an' if it's somethin' wild they can tie it up."

This seemed to the Outlaws an excellent solution of the problem, and William went indoors to write out the notice. Soon he emerged carrying it and wearing the complacent smile of successful authorship.

"Here it is," he said with modest pride. "All right, isn't it?"

They gathered round to look. It read as follows:

"mister william brown is going to lekcher on anmals and will be gratful to anyone who will give or lend him anmals to be lekchered on mister william brown will take grate care of them mister william brown is out now lookin for valubul insex but will be back before dinner mister william brown will be glad if people givin him anmals to be lekchered on will put them on the seat in the back garden an tie them up if they are savvidge anmals cause of doin damidge an eatin things reely wild anmals should have cages as mister william browns father will be mad with him if dammidge is done to the garden by wild animals lent or given him for his lekcher if anmals are lent him will they kinly have a label with the address of their home so as mister william brown the lekcherer on anmals may bring them home after they have been lekchered on things like hedgehogs or porkquipines must be fetched mister william brown is a very interestin lekcherer an anyone may kinly come an listen to him who likes if the summerhouse is full peple may come an look at him thru the window."

The other Outlaws were less impressed by this than was its author. Ginger voiced their feelings.

"Good deal about you in it," he commented, "an' not much about us."

"Well, who's the lecturer?" demanded William with spirit, "me or you?"

"Yes," said Ginger, "an' who works jus' as hard as you *or* harder gettin' things ready?"

William soothed their feelings by adding a footnote to his notice:

"mister william browns vallubal assistunts are ginger and douglas."

Conciliated by this they helped William to pin the notice on the side gate and sallied forth with him in search of insects.

A short time before their return, Hector appeared looking very hot and breathless. He held a parrot in a cage. He had cycled frenziedly into the nearest town for it and he had spent practically his last penny on it. He came round to the back of the house. Ethel's window was, he believed, at the back of the house. There he found a garden seat conveniently situated. He put the parrot upon that and tiptoed to the side door. He had decided to do the whole graceful action as Ethel's friend's friend had done it. If Ethel was touched at second hand, as it were, by the action as performed by her friend's friend, how much more would she be

"WHO'S THE LECTURER?" DEMANDED WILLIAM WITH SPIRIT. "ME OR YOU?"

touched when it was actually done to her.

He slipped a letter quietly through the letter-box. In the letter he said that if she would look out of the window she would see upon the garden seat a little friend who had come to keep her company. Then, still hot and breathless, but smiling fatuously to himself, he tiptoed away.

Hardly had he disappeared when the Outlaws returned. The expedition had not been, upon the whole, a great success. They had only found one species of caterpillar that William did not already possess. They carried it carefully in a little tin which contained also a large amount of greenery for its nourishment.

"Well, we've not found *much*," said Douglas despondently.

"No," said William, "but—but someone might've brought an animal for us while we've been away."

"Yes, an' they mightn't," said Douglas. "I bet you anythin' that we find that ole garden seat as empty as we left it."

"An' I bet we find somethin' put on it," said William with gallant but unconvinced optimism.

They turned the corner of the house and stood there transfixed for a moment with rapture and amazement.

There upon the garden seat was a parrot in a cage.

Recovering from their paralysis they rushed to it and bore it off in triumph to the summer-house.

"*Well*," said William deeply touched and with his faith in human nature entirely restored. "I do call that decent of *somebody*."

"An' no labels on," said Ginger, "that means we can keep it. They've *given* it."

They crowded round their acquisition, still half incredulous of their amazing good fortune.

"Someone must've come down the lane an' seen the

notice," said William, "an' then gone home to fetch their parrot to give us. P'raps it'd belonged to some relation what'd died an' they din't know what to do with it or p'raps"—hopefully—"it uses such bad language that they din't like to have it in the house."

As if intensely amused by the idea the parrot uttered a shrill scream of laughter and when its paroxysm of mirth was over said with deep feeling: "Go away. I hate you."

This so delighted the Outlaws that they crowded round it again hoping it would repeat it, but though it would whistle and make the sound of a cork coming out of a bottle and utter a most offensive snigger, it refused to oblige the Outlaws by telling them again that it hated them.

"Wonder what they eat," said Ginger still gazing enraptured at their new pet.

"Well, don't you start givin' it any of your berries," said William sternly. Then looking round: "I say where's that tin with my caterpillar in? Who's took it?"

"You left it on the garden seat when we fetched the parrot in," said Douglas, "I saw you."

They hurried out to the garden seat.

It was empty.

"Well, of all the *cheek*," said William indignantly, "someone's pinched it."

"Never mind it," said Ginger, "we've got a parrot. What's a caterpillar when we've got a parrot?"

"I *want* that caterpillar," said William doggedly, "I'd thought of a lot of things to say about it an' I'm goin' to get another. Come on. Let's shut up the parrot in the summer-house where no one can steal it an' all go out to look for another caterpillar."

Without much enthusiasm they agreed.

"An' what I'd like to know," said William darkly, "is where that caterpillar *is*."

That caterpillar was a matter of fact in Ethel's bedroom, being flung, tin box and all, into the fireplace in a fit of temper. A housemaid had found Hector's note on the mat and taken it up to Ethel's room. Ethel's room did not happen to overlook the garden. She read the note with a smile almost as fatuous as Hector's. She remembered what she had told them about the parrot. Suppose he'd remembered the story and brought her a parrot. "A little friend to keep you company." . . . It might, of course, be a kitten or a puppy. . . . Anyway, it was very, very sweet of him. She opened her door and, still smiling, called to the housemaid who was sweeping the stairs.

"Emma, will you go out and bring me something that you'll find upon the garden seat."

Emma went out and returned with a small tin. Ethel's smile faded.

"Was this all that there was upon the garden seat?" she asked.

"Yes, miss. There was nothing else."

Ethel returned to her room and opened the tin. Inside were several leaves and a big furry caterpillar. There was nothing else.

"Oh, *that's* his idea of being funny, is it?" said Ethel viciously. "Well, it's not *mine*."

And it was then that she flung the tin furiously into the fireplace.

At that very moment had she but known it, the faithful George was tiptoeing softly round the house bearing a parrot in a cage. He too was hot and breathless. He too had cycled into the neighbouring market town for the parrot. He too had spent practically his last penny on it. He too had decided to leave it on the garden seat and drop into the letter box a note about a "little friend to keep her company." He entered the back garden. There was a convenient garden seat. He put down the cage upon it, slipped his note into the letter box and went home smiling to himself. How pleased she'd be about it. . . . It would give him a pull over that ass Hector. Near the gate he met the Outlaws carrying a tin. They passed each other as usual without any sign of recognition. Both Ginger and Hector and Douglas and George, whatever stage of cordiality or the reverse their relations might have attained at home, made it a point of honour to pass each other on the public highway as if they had never seen each other before. At present relations at home were not cordial.

"Smilin'," muttered Douglas bitterly when he had passed. "Yes, 's all right for *him* to go about smilin' —takin' people's mouth-organs off them an' ru'nin' them."

"Funny we only caught one of those caterpillars again," said William meditatively.

"Well, one's enough to lecture on, I suppose," said Douglas rather irritably. The sight of the fatuously smiling George had reminded him of his grievances. "I'd like to see someone take somethin' of *his* away," he went on, little knowing how literally his wish was to be fulfilled.

"An' I'd saved up for that trumpet," said Ginger. "I don't s'pose I'll ever—what's the matter?"

William, who was walking in front, had stopped suddenly on turning the corner of the house and was staring in blank amazement, eyes and mouth wide open.

"There—there's another parrot on the seat," he said faintly. "Seems—seems sort of impossible but—look!"

They looked. Like William's, their eyes and mouth opened wide in blank amazement.

"It is, isn't it?" said William still faintly as if he

couldn't quite believe his eyes. "It *is* another parrot, isn't it?"

"Yes," said Ginger also rather faintly, "it cert'nly is. Someone else must've passed the notice. Seems sort of funny they should *all* be givin' us parrots, dun't it?"

With a certain dazed bewilderment beneath their ecstasy the Outlaws approached this new "gift."

"Let's take it in the summer-house an' see if it talks to the other," said William.

They took it into the summer-house and the other parrot greeted it with a sardonic laugh. The latest comer gazed round the summer-house with a supercilious air and finally ejaculated "Great Scott!"

Ginger drew a breath of delight but William, in whom familiarity with parrots was breeding contempt and who was becoming over critical, merely said, "If that's the worst bad language it knows it's not goin' to be very int'restin'." Then he looked about him. "Where's that tin with the caterpillar in?"

"You left it on the bench again, William," said Douglas.

They went out and stood around the empty bench.

"*Well*," said William "it's—it's mos' *mysterious*. Someone's pinched *this* one too."

Upstairs Ethel was hurling the second caterpillar and tin furiously into the fireplace.

"Very funny, aren't they?" she was saying. "'A little friend to keep you company.' And two caterpillars. Oh, yes, it's a *great* joke, isn't it. All *right*, my young friends, all *right*."

"Well, all I can say *is*," William was saying, "that it's one of the mos' *mysterious* things what've ever happened to me in all my life. Two parrots give me an' two tins of caterpillars stole off me in the same mornin' . . . but 's no good goin' out to find another now.

There's not time. We'll jus' have to have the lecture without it."

*   *   *

It was late afternoon. Hector, still wearing his fatuous smile, came round the corner of the house. He'd expected a note of thanks before now. He felt that he couldn't wait a minute longer without hearing an account of Ethel's rapturous glee on the receipt of his present. He could imagine it, of course, but he wanted to hear someone telling him about it. "She was delighted" . . . "So kind of you" . . . "She was *deeply* touched" . . . "She's writing to you now" . . . "She's longing for the time when her quarantine will be over and she can see you and thank you properly," . . . were a few of the phrases that occurred to him. . . .

A housemaid opened the door.

"I just—er—called to see if the parrot was settling down all right," said Hector in an ingratiating manner.

"The parrot?" said the housemaid in surprise.

"Yes, the parrot that arrived this morning."

"No parrot arrived this morning, sir," said the housemaid.

It was Hector's turn to be surprised.

"W-what?" he said, "are—are you sure."

"Quite sure, sir," said the housemaid. "There's no parrot in the house at all."

"Not—er—not in Miss Brown's room," said Hector desperately.

"No, sir, I've just been there."

Dazedly Hector walked away. Of course the thing was as plain as daylight. What a fool he'd been to leave the thing out there on the seat. Some tramp had come back to the back door and run off with it. And he'd spent all the money he'd got on it. . . . Wasn't it the *rottenest*——

He stopped and stared. He'd wandered disconsolately round to the other side of the house and there, just outside the closed door of the summer-house, stood William with a parrot in a cage.

* * *

The lecture was over. The Outlaws had collected a small and unruly audience of children who'd nothing else to do but no one had enjoyed it except William, who had lectured to his own entire satisfaction and was now feeling tired and hoarse. He was, moreover, beginning to find his parrots more of a liability than an asset. All attempts at closer acquaintance with them had been resisted so promptly that both Ginger and Douglas had had to improvise bandages for bleeding fingers from very grimy handkerchiefs, and William's nose had been bitten almost in two while he was gazing fondly at his new possessions through the bars. Also there was the economic side of the question to consider. William had been down to the village to ascertain the price of parrot food and had come back aghast at the result.

"We simply can't afford to keep 'em," he said.

"Well, I know I can't. I'd have nothin' left for myself at all out of the bit of pocket money they give me."

"Can't they live on scraps an' things?" said Ginger.

"Oh, yes," said William, "I guess you'd like to try feedin' 'em on pois'nous berries same as what you did with the dormouse."

"Well, it was mine, wasn't it?" said Ginger with spirit.

"Yes, but *this* isn't," said William, "this was given me to lecture on an' I'm not goin' to have it killed with pois'nous berries by you."

"What are you goin' to do with it, then?" said Ginger, "if you say you can't buy it proper food?"

"I don't know yet," said William irritably.

Like most other lecturers he was suffering the reaction from his expenditure of eloquence.

At this point the two parrots began to hold a screaming contest till William was forced to take George's outside and close the door, whereupon the clamour died down. It was at this moment that Hector came round the corner of the house. His first impulse was to hurl himself upon William and accuse him of stealing his parrot. But on approaching nearer he saw that it was not his parrot. It was not his parrot and it was not his cage. His expression changed. He approached William in a manner that can only be described as ingratiating.

"Whose is that parrot, William?" he asked pleasantly.

"Mine," said William shortly.

"W-where did you get it?" said Hector still more pleasantly.

"Someone gave it to me," said William.

There was a short silence, then Hector said slowly:

"I was just wanting a parrot like that."

"Were you?" said William.

Hector cleared his throat and then said in a manner that was more ingratiating than ever:

"They're rather dangerous, you know, and very expensive to feed.'

William secretly agreed with both these statements, but he gave no sign of having even heard them. A shade of nervousness crept into Hector's ingratiating manner.

"I—I'm willing to buy that parrot from you, William," he offered.

William turned a steady eye upon him.

"How much for?" he said sternly.

Hector hesitated. He hadn't any money to speak of. With a different type of child, of course, one might——

He'd always disliked William far more than the other Outlaws.

"They're not expensive things, of course," he said carelessly, hoping that William did not know their value, "and they're a lot of trouble. One must take into account that they're delicate birds and one has to——"

William interrupted. A sudden gleam had come into William's eye.

"I tell you what I'll do," he said, "I'll swop it with you."

"What for?" said Hector hopefully.

The gleam in William's eye became brighter, more steely.

"I want to give Ginger a present," he said carelessly. "I want to give him one of those nice trumpets. The *very* nice ones. You can get 'em at Foley's in the village. They cost six shillings. I'll swop it with you for one of those trumpets to give to Ginger."

William's freckled face was absolutely expressionless as he made this offer. For a minute there was murder in Hector's eye. He went purple, controlled himself with an effort, then after a minute's silence full of unspoken words, gulped and said:

"Very well. You wait here."

Soon he was back with the trumpet. He hurled it at William with a gesture of anger and contempt, seized the parrot cage and disappeared. He was going to take it home, write a beautiful little note, fasten it to the ring, and deliver it in person at the front door. He wasn't going to repeat his mistake of leaving it anywhere where it could be stolen before it reached the beloved's hands.

Inside the summer-house the Outlaws were dancing a dance of exultation and triumph around Ginger who was producing loud but discordant strains from his magnificent new trumpet.

This festive gathering was, however, broken by the sudden advent of George who, like Hector, had not been able to resist the temptation of coming round to receive a detailed description of Ethel's delight. Like Hector he had been informed that no parrot had entered the house that day. He had then caught a glimpse of the Outlaws in the summer-house leaping wildly about a parrot in a cage to the mingled strains of some devilish musical instrument and the shrill sardonic chuckles of a parrot. He hurled himself in upon them in fury.

"You little *thieves*," he panted, seizing William by both ears. "What do you *mean* by taking my parrot?"

William firmly but with great dignity freed his ears, then as firmly and with as much dignity replied:

" 'S not your parrot, 'S ours."

George looked at the parrot and his jaw dropped. William was right. It wasn't his parrot. It wasn't his cage.

He gulped. His anger departed. A certain propitiatory note came into his voice as he began to make tentative enquiries as to the exact value William set upon his parrot. It appeared that though William valued his parrot very highly indeed, still in order to oblige George he was willing to exchange it for a mouth-organ, one of the six-shilling ones from Foley's, because he happened to want to give one to Douglas as a present. George, after displaying all the symptoms of an imminent apoplectic fit, went off to buy the mouth-organ, returned with it, flung it furiously at the Outlaws and stalked off with his parrot.

William turned to the other Outlaws.

"I mus' say," he admitted, "that a lot of extraordinary things seem to be hap'nin' to us to-day. People givin' away parrots an' other people wantin' 'em an'—let's go'n' see what he's goin' to do with it."

At a discreet distance they followed George round

and out of the side gate. George was going to take the parrot in at the front door, ring the bell, and deliver it in person. He wasn't going to run the risk of having it stolen a second time. . . . And then, to his amazement, he saw Hector blithely approaching from the opposite direction also carrying a parrot in a cage. Hector had been home, had written a graceful little note, attached it to the ring of the cage, and was now coming to present it to Ethel. They met at the gate. Their mouths slowly opened. Their eyes bulged in fury and amazement as each recognised his own parrot and cage in the hand of the other. Simultaneously they shouted "So *you* stole my parrot."

The Outlaws watched in mystified delight. A shabby-looking man who happened to be passing also stopped to form an interested audience.

"It's not your parrot . . . I say *you* stole mine."

"I did *not* . . . *that's* my parrot you're holding."

"You heard her say she'd like a parrot and you——"

"You couldn't afford one yourself so you pinched mine and——"

"A jolly good thing I've caught you——"

"I did *not*——"

"You *did*——"

"You're a liar and a thief."

"I'm not. You are."

"I'm what?"

"A liar and a thief."

"Say that again."

"A liar and a thief."

"Are you referring to me or to you?"

"To you."

"Well, say it again."

"You're a liar and a thief."

Feeling words inadequate, but finding the cage he was

carrying an impediment to threatening gestures, George turned round, thrust it into William's arms with a curt "take that" and began to roll up his sleeves. Hector turned to the shabby-looking man, who stood just behind him, thrust his cage into his arms, and began to roll up his sleeves. The next minute George and Hector, who attended the same boxing class and knew each other's style by heart, were giving a splendid display upon the high road, with bare fists. From the *mélange* came at regular intervals the words "thief" and "liar," "you did," "I didn't."

It was clear that in the shabby-looking man's breast there raged a struggle between duty and pleasure—the pleasure of watching the fight and the duty of providing for himself the necessities of life. Duty won, and he crept softly away with his parrot and cage, and was never seen or heard of in that locality again.

William stood for a minute deep in thought, then went quietly indoors with his parrot and cage, leaving Hector and George still deaf and blind to everything but the joy of fighting.

William, still very thoughtful, carried his cage up to Ethel's room.

"I won't come in, Ethel," he said softly, "'cause of catching your quarantine illness, but I've brought you a little present. I heard you'd said you'd like a parrot an' I've brought you one."

Ethel and his mother came to the door and stared at him in amazement. Freckled, stern, inscrutable, he handed the cage to Ethel.

"B-but wherever did you get it, William?" said Mrs. Brown.

"A man gave it to me," said William.

"A *man* gave it to you?" gasped Mrs. Brown.

"Yes," said William, his face and voice entirely

devoid of any expression. "A man in the road gave it me. He just put it in my arms an' said: 'Take that.' He gave it me."

"*Well!*" gasped Mrs. Brown, "isn't that *extraordinary!* But there *are* a lot of eccentric people about and"—vaguely—"one's always reading of queer things in the newspapers."

Ethel was deeply touched. That William should bring his present straight to her. That it should be William who remembered her lightly expressed wish for a parrot which those two—well, there weren't any words strong enough for them—had only ridiculed. . . . She felt drawn to William as never before.

"How—how *very* kind of you, William," she said. "I—you can have your bow and arrow back. I'm sorry I took if from you. It's—it's *very* kind of you to bring me the parrot."

William received his bow and arrow with perfunctory thanks. Just at that moment the housemaid came up with a note. Ethel tore it open.

"Why, it's all right," she said. "Daphne hasn't got measles after all. The rash has all gone, and the doctor says she's not got it at all, and they want me to go to tea, and they've got that artist coming—you know, the one that said that I was the loveliest girl he'd ever seen in his life, and—— Oh, how jolly. I'll start at once."

"May Douglas and Ginger and me walk with you just as far as there, Ethel?" said William.

"Certainly, William," said Ethel in her melted mood.

A few minutes later Ethel, accompanied by William, Ginger and Douglas, set out fron the front door. William carried his bow and arrow, Ginger his magnificent new trumpet, and Douglas his magnificent new mouth-organ. They walked very jauntily.

At the gate Hector and George came forward to greet

them. The fight was just over. It had been indecisive. They were equally matched and knew each other's style of boxing too well ever to be taken by surprise, so the

ETHEL PASSED THE TWO YOUNG MEN, HEAD IN AIR, WITHOUT ANY SIGN OF RECOGNITION. WILLIAM WAVED HIS BOW AND ARROW IN IRONIC FAREWELL.

fight had finally been abandoned by mutual consent. At the unexpected sight of Ethel emerging from the front door escorted by the Outlaws, they pulled themselves together and hastened forward with smiles of greeting.

Ethel passed them head in air without any sign of recognition. They stood gaping after her in helpless bewilderment. The Outlaws turned back to look at

GEORGE AND HECTOR STOOD GAZING IN HELPLESS BEWILDERMENT.

them, Ginger and Douglas raised trumpet and mouth-organ to their lips and uttered defiant strains, William waved his bow and arrow in careless greeting, then they turned back and went on their way accompanying Ethel, an indescribable swagger in their walk.

George and Hector picked up their hats from the dust

and walked slowly away in the opposite direction.

* * *

Ethel wasn't in quarantine after all. And she was going out to tea to meet the artist who said she was the loveliest girl he'd ever seen in his life. She was tired to death of those two boys but—but it was all right now.

She was perfectly happy.

* * *

The Outlaws had got back their confiscated property, and then some, as they say across the Atlantic. They had scored most gloriously off their enemies. They had had a most successful day. There had been, it is true, certain mysterious elements in it that they could not understand, but that did not matter. It had been a most successful day. They were perfectly happy.

* * *

George and Hector walked down the road arm in arm. Their conflict had stimulated them and roused again all their old friendship. They were confiding in each other that women were unreliable and incalculable and that it was best to give them a wide berth. They were congratulating each other on the narrow escape from the lifelong unhappiness that marriage with Ethel would have meant to them.

Then they went on to discuss the latest football results.

They were perfectly happy. . . .

Chapter 7

One Good Turn

The atmosphere in William's home was electric, or, as William put it, everyone seemed to be in a bait but him. Uncle Frederick was staying with them, and not only Uncle Frederick but also a distant cousin, many times removed, called Flavia. Flavia is a romantic name, but not as romantic as its owner. Flavia was tall and slim and dark with deep violet eyes. Not that William thought she was romantic. He did not even realise that she was tall and slim and dark with deep violet eyes. To William she was merely an ordinary and quite unattractive grown-up. He had tested her intelligence and found it entirely lacking (she did not, for instance, know the difference between a Poplar Hawk and a Vaporer, nor did she take the slightest interest in the records of his prize "conker"). He felt in her, however, the aloof impersonal interest he felt for all the girls whom Robert admired. For Robert admired Flavia. At sight of her he had forgotten all his other ladye loves (and they had been numerous), had forgotten even that he had always intended to marry a small girl with golden hair and blue eyes, and had gazed on her even while the introduction was taking place with a lovelorn gaze that riveted William's attention at once. William liked to keep up with Robert's love affairs, and on account of their fleeting nature, this was less easy than it sounds. As he watched the introduction he mentally transferred the focus of Robert's affection from the golden-haired girl he'd been taking on the river last week to this new arrival. He was on the whole relieved to find her devoid of intelligence. It always vaguely shocked him to find intelligence—a knowledge of insects or interest in conker battles—in inamoratas of Robert's. It seemed such a waste of it.

It might be supposed that the course of true love would run very smooth indeed with the inamorata beneath the same roof, but it didn't. It didn't because of Uncle Frederick. Uncle Frederick needed a perpetual audience. Uncle Frederick accompanied Flavia and Robert wherever they went. He insisted on walking in the middle and he talked all the time. He talked about his stamp collection. He had a collection of ten thousand stamps, and he was never perfectly happy except when he was talking about them. He knew his collection by heart and he could describe each one of them in detail. He could—in fact he did—talk about his collection for hours and hours and hours and hours without stopping. He took for granted that Robert and Flavia liked to have him with them wherever they went and so he always went with them. He went for walks with them. He went for picnics with them. He went on the river with them. He went out to tea with them. He played tennis with them. He sat in the garden with them. And always he talked to them about his stamp collection. Sometimes in the evening he read aloud to them from a book called "The Joy of Stamp Collecting."

They were sitting on a seat in the garden—Uncle Frederick in the middle, Robert and Flavia on either side.

"I wish you could see it," Uncle Frederick was saying;

"it's quite an unique collection. Did I ever tell you how I got that Japanese stamp?"

"Yes," said Robert gloomily.

Robert had an uneasy suspicion that he could see William's face through the laurel bushes, framed in its feathered Indian head-dress, wearing its unholy grin.

"I'd like to have brought the collection with me," went on Uncle Frederick, "but of course it's very large and cumbersome. And I'm afraid of thieves. It's extraordinary how thieves do get to hear of these things, and of course they're very cunning. Did I tell you about the man I met who'd had a very rare complete set of Italian stamps taken out of his pocket-book during a journey without feeling anything?"

"Yes," said Robert.

Uncle Frederick threw him a suspicious glance. He was almost sure he'd never told Robert that story. Slightly disconcerted, he paused a minute, then pulling himself together continued: "I keep them at home in a specially constructed safe. It would, I think, baffle any burglar, but of course they are very cunning. I never come away like this without feeling anxious about my stamps. The first thing I do when I get home is to go my safe and ascertain that they are all there. Did I ever tell you——" He stopped, glanced at Robert and began the sentence again. "I remember hearing of a man once who had a most valuable collection stolen and faked stamps put in its stead. It was some months before he discovered the trick."

Robert leant over to Flavia who sat serene in the consciousness of her beauty, and, assuming an expression which caused much delight to the hidden William—an expression which soulless people sometimes compare to that of "a dying duck in a thunder-storm"—said:

"Would you like to come to the summer-house,

Flavia? There's a very pretty view of the rose garden from there."

"Certainly," said Flavia demurely as she rose.

"You stay here, Uncle Frederick," said Robert hastily, seeing that Uncle Frederick, too, was rising, and added solicitously, "I'm sure you're tired with our walk this morning. You rest here while I show Flavia the view from the summer-house."

"Oh, no," said Uncle Frederick briskly, "I'm not at all tired; I'm a very good walker. I could outwalk you both, I dare say. I'll come and look at this view from the summer-house with you. I remember there was a summer-house at home when I was a boy. I used to take my stamp collection down there to arrange them. I remember that it was in the old summer-house that I added the last of the complete set of Austrian stamps to my collection. A friend of my father gave it to me, and I took it down to the summer-house to put it into my album."

The three of them wended their way to the summer-house. William, wearing his Red Indian costume, followed through the bushes. He found the expression on Robert's face highly diverting.

They stood in the summer-house, Uncle Frederick in the middle, Robert and Flavia on either side, William discreetly peeping through a crack in the side.

"Well, where's this view from the summer-house?" said Uncle Frederick.

"There," said Robert savagely. Uncle Frederick looked through the little window.

"It doesn't seem to me," he said, "much different from the view you get from the house."

Robert ground his teeth.

"I don't see anything at all specially attractive about the view of the rose garden from this particular spot," went on Uncle Frederick. "However—we each have our own standard of beauty, and what appeals to one does not appeal to all. I know quite a lot of people, for instance, who judge stamps entirely by their artistic appearance, quite irrespective of their value. Did I ever tell you of the lady who——?"

"Yes," interrupted Robert viciously. Uncle Frederick looked at him coldly.

"I don't think I did," he said. "You must be thinking of some other story I told you. This lady was forming a stamp collection and I told her that she could choose any stamp she liked on a certain page of my album (not one containing my most valuable stamps, of course) to form the nucleus of her collection, and she chose one of no value at all just because she liked the picture on it."

Robert leaned over to Flavia again.

"Would you care to come and see the greenhouse," he said, "and look at the—er—carnations?"

"Certainly," said Flavia pleasantly, rising.

"We'll be back with you in a minute, Uncle," said Robert hastily, seeing that Uncle Frederick was rising, too.

"Oh, I'll come and look at the carnations," said Uncle Frederick. "I'm very much interested in carnations. And very unusual, too, for them to be out this time of the year."

The three of them went on to the greenhouse and stood there, Uncle Frederick in the middle, Robert and Flavia on either side. Uncle Frederick looked about him.

"Well," he said, "where are the carnations? I don't see any carnations."

"I didn't mean carnations," said Robert desperately, "I meant," he swept his arm wildly round the greenhouse, "I meant these."

"These," Uncle Frederick adjusted his spectacles and

began to look around. "I see . . . Begonias. Very nice, very nice. I'm glad you thought of showing us these, Robert. I'm very fond of begonias, aren't you, Flavia?"

Robert, standing behind his uncle, bared his lips in a silent and impotent snarl of fury. It was at that moment that he espied William's feather-encircled head gazing through one of the glass panes with a smile of quiet enjoyment. He turned the snarl of fury on to William. William promptly disappeared. Uncle Frederick turned abruptly and caught the tail-end of the snarl of fury. He looked startled and concerned.

"Are you in pain, my poor boy?" he said.

"No," said Robert, "I mean yes. I mean, not much."

"I'm afraid you've been over-doing it," he said. "Flavia, we've tired out our young friend, I'm afraid. The walk was too much for him. I suspect that he indulges in too much physical exercise and too little mental recreation. You should collect stamps, my boy. There's nothing like it. Have I ever told you how I came to collect stamps?"

"No," said Robert. "I mean yes. Yes, you have."

At that minute the first lunch gong sounded.

"I'll tell you about the origin of my stamp collection afterwards. Let us now follow yon welcome sound."

Groaning inwardly, Robert followed it. He stalked angrily into the dining-room and flung himself into the nearest chair. It was unfortunate that William had been into the room a minute before and had carelessly flung down his Red Indian head-dress upon that very chair, and that at the end of the head-dress was the unguarded pin that had secured it around William's head. Robert leapt into the air with a high-pitched cry of agony, which swiftly changed to a growl of fury when he saw the cause of his involuntary ascent. The sight of the head-dress reminded him, too, of the unholy grin on William's face as it peered in at the greenhouse, rejoicing in his discomfiture. With a gesture of rage he flung the whole thing into the fire. That to a small extent—a very small extent—relieved his feelings, so that when William entered a few minutes later, still wearing his frilled khaki trousers and looked around with a stern "Where's my feather thing?" Robert could answer with great dignity and nonchalance: "In the fire."

"Who put it there?" said William.

"I did," said Robert.

William's face grew stern and lowering, but he said nothing.

"You shouldn't leave it about all over the place," said Robert.

"Did you sit on the pin?" said William with sudden hope.

But Robert refused to allow him even that gleam of comfort.

"Course I didn't," he said.

"I bet you did," said William, "an' let me tell *you*. There's not many people'd dare to throw away a Red Indian head thing. At least," he ended darkly, "not without knowin' somethin'd happen to them."

With this sinister threat he withdrew, to put his head round the door a few minutes later, having thought of something else to say.

"You needn't be so mad at *me*," he said. "*I've* not been goin' round with you all mornin' talkin' about my stamp collection. Why don' you throw one of *his* hats in the fire?"

And withdrew before Robert could get hold of anything to throw at him.

* * *

They met in the barn. William, Ginger, Douglas and

Joan. They all wore their Red Indian dresses. Joan—the only female Outlaw—had a squaw-dress which she had made herself and which made up in ornamentation what it lacked in cut and unobtrusiveness of stitching. Its ornamentation was little short of reckless. She had sewn the entire contents of twelve penny boxes of beads on to it. All of them—Joan openly, the Outlaws secretly—were intensely proud of it. All except William wore feathered head-dresses. Briefly William told the story of its disappearance.

"He oughter know it's a *serious* thing," he said, "throwin' Red Indian chief's feathers into the fire. It's a *ninsult*. He's lucky I'm not a *real* Red Indian or he'd be scalped. That's what he deserves. He deserves to be scalped—throwin' Red Indian chief's head things into the fire."

They set out for the wood where they had agreed to "scout" each other, but William's gloomy sense of outraged honour threw a shadow over all of them. In vain for Ginger, Douglas, Henry and Joan to comment brightly on the fine day or the prospect of a good scouting expedition. In vain for each of them to offer to lend him his own head-dress. In reply William muttered, "He's jolly lucky not to be scalped, that's what he is. I bet if any *real* Red Indian knew he'd done it, he'd come over an' scalp him."

They began to walk over the field that led to the wood where their scouting expedition was to take place. Suddenly Joan stopped. "Look!" she said. "A fairy ring!" William snorted scornfully and strode on. "Oh, but it is," said Joan, "do come and look at it."

They stopped to look at a little circle of toadstools in the green grass.

"Well, what of it?" said William, determined not to be impressed.

"What is it?" said Ginger.

"It's a fairy ring," said Joan, "if you stand in the middle and wish, your wish comes true."

William emitted again his famous snort of contempt and derision.

"It does," persisted Joan. "Honestly. The last time I came across one I stood in the middle and wished there'd be trifle for dinner and there was."

The Outlaws were despite themselves impressed by this. William, however, merely said:

"Oh, yes, we've had enough of your fairy stuff. Do you remember the ole donkey what——"

"But, William," said Joan. "It couldn't do any harm just to wish something."

"All right," said William.

He stepped into the fairy ring.

"I wish a real Indian Chief'd come alone an' scalp Robert for burnin' my head thing," he said.

Then they all proceeded except Ginger, who stepped hastily into the ring and silently wished that there might be roast turkey, strawberries and cream and trifle and ice cream for supper. He was aware that this was very unlikely, but he was optimistic and thought it worth trying.

* * *

William had almost forgotten his grievance when he returned home for tea. His mother was out, but Uncle Frederick was having tea with Robert and Flavia.

"Apart from its historical and geographical interest it's such a wonderful investment," Uncle Frederick was saying. "I know of a stamp which sold for four pounds in 1898 and which sells for over fifteen pounds to-day."

Robert cleared his throat. He had long ago relinquished subtle methods in trying to oust Uncle

Frederick's stamps from the conversation and introduce his own topics.

"I made a wireless set last month," he said.

"Great Britain 1840," said Uncle Frederick.

"Seven valves," said Robert.

"Black V. R.," said Uncle Frederick.

"I can get Germany," said Robert.

Flavia merely sat by as usual serenely conscious of her beauty.

Uncle Frederick despite himself yielded to Robert's determined egotism.

"A what?" he said, "a wireless set?"

"Yes," said Robert, glancing at Flavia to make sure that she was listening. "I made it myself. Seven valves. I can get anywhere with it."

"Strange as it may seem," said Uncle Frederick, "I have never listened to one of those instruments—'listened in' is, I believe, the correct expression. As it happens I do not possess one myself, nor do any of my friends. Nor have I ever wished to purchase one. As an entertainment I do not consider that it even approaches stamp collecting. But still—I see that it might be interesting. The news, for instance—the weather forecast—that is given every night, I believe."

William, considering that he had been left out of the conversation long enough and seeing an opportunity of entering into it, swallowed half a bun unmasticated and burst out:

"Yes, it's giv'n every night, but it's nothin' to go by. The weather forecast, I mean. If it says it's goin' to rain it gen'rally doesn't, and if it says it isn't, it gen'rally does." He caught Robert's eye fixed on him sternly, with an expression that could only mean that he was going to eject him mercilessly from the conversation at the first opportunity, and returning the gaze defiantly continued in a loud voice: "The weather forecast comes first an' then the S.O.S's. and then——"

"S.O.S.?" said Uncle Frederick, "and what is that?"

"Oh, it's telling people away from home when they're wanted at home," said William vaguely. "Tellin' 'em you know when somethin's gone wrong an' they've gotter go home at once."

Uncle Frederick seemed much impressed.

"I see," he said, "an excellent idea. A means of getting into touch at once with anyone who is absent. An excellent idea. I see. Then——"

"Seven valves," said Robert at last, forcing his way back into the conversation, talking to Uncle Frederick and gazing at the serene and beautiful Flavia, "seven valves—a much larger number than most sets are made with. It took me a very long time to make it. I——"

William, realising that all further attempts on his part at getting back into the conversation would be firmly thwarted by Robert, put one bun into his mouth, slipped another into his pocket and quietly departed.

The indignity of having had his Indian head-dress destroyed still rankled in William's breast, but it was growing dimmer with the passage of time. He made his way to a neighbouring farm and there made a collection of hens' feathers to form a new and yet more splendid head-band. He then took them to a wood near by to count and he was engaged thus when to his amazement and dismay he beheld a Red Indian Chief in full panoply approaching him through the wood. He rubbed his eyes to make sure that it was true and not a vision. It was true. A tall man with a red, hawk-nosed face, an enormous head-dress of feathers, wearing magnificent Red Indian panoply, was stalking past him through the wood in the direction of the road that led to William's house. It was amazing. But there it was. It was true. And suddenly he

A RED INDIAN CHIEF IN FULL PANOPLY WAS APPROACHING WILLIAM THROUGH THE WOOD.

remembered his wish in the fairy ring—that a real Red Indian Chief should come and scalp Robert. His heart sank down to his shoes. Crumbs! This was more than he'd bargained for! *Crumbs!* He'd no idea—— He gazed at the vision with awe and astonishment and growing

WILLIAM GAZED AT THE VISION WITH ASTONISHMENT AND HORROR. CRUMBS! THIS WAS MORE THAN HE'D BARGAINED FOR!

horror. He could not, of course, know that the vision was an acquaintance of Robert's who had arranged to call for Robert on his way to a small fancy dress party to which they were both going. Robert had as a matter of fact carefully hidden from William his intention of going to the fancy dress party, on the general principle that the less William knew of his movements the better. William roused himself from his paralysis and rose trembling to intercept the stranger.

"Where you goin'?" he demanded tremulously.

"To The Hollies," said the stranger.

William's heart sank yet deeper. The Hollies was the name of William's house.

"Who—who you goin' there for?" he faltered.

"For Robert Brown," said the stranger.

It was true. William moistened his lips.

"What you goin' to do to Robert?" he said faintly.

The stranger looked down. He liked making fun of small boys.

"Scalp him," he answered with a dramatic snarl, and began again to stride through the wood. William hurried along trying to keep pace with him.

"Look here," he said breathlessly. "I didn't mean it. Honest, I didn't. I didn't know there was anythin' in it. Honest, I didn't. I don' want you to do it, really. I mean, I c'n make a new one an' I don' really mind now. P'raps he sat on the pin an' then threw it into the fire without thinkin' what he was doin'. Look here, if you go back where you came from——"

"What on earth do you mean?" demanded the stranger striding onwards.

"You—you can't go to Robert," said William desperately. " 'S'no use goin' for him. You won't find him. He's not at home."

"Where is he?" demanded the stranger.

William was silent for a moment, searching in his mind for some place whither a Red Indian, lusting for vengeance, could not follow.

At last:

"He's gone up in an aeroplane," he said, "an' none of us know when he's comin' down, so it's no use you waitin' for him."

At this moment Robert, dressed in a Harlequin costume, issued from a side gate and hailed his friend.

"Hallo," he said, "you're in jolly good time, and, by Jove, you do look fine!"

William, with a snort of disgust, turned on his heel.

Robert's friend watched his retreating figure.

"Who's that?" he said.

"My brother," said Robert.

"Is he potty?" said the friend. "He just said you'd gone up in an aeroplane."

"Oh, yes, he's as potty as they make 'em," said Robert carelessly.

Robert had been uncertain whether to go to the fancy dress party or not. Had there been any chance of spending the evening alone with Flavia, he would, of course, not have gone, but Uncle Frederick had announced his intention of reading aloud to Flavia and him a little pamphlet he had just bought called "The Romance of Stamp Collecting." So in disgust Robert went with his friend to the fancy dress party. And the next morning he carelessly threw to William the most magnificent feathered head-dress William had ever seen.

"That chap who went with me last night gave me that," he said; "he'd got two and didn't want this one, so he gave it to me. You can have it."

It is probable that very mixed motives had prompted Robert's gift. It is possible that he felt some compunction of heart at his impulsive destruction of William's treasured head-dress. It is more than possible that he felt apprehensive as to the results. He knew that people did not as a rule insult William with impunity. He had been as a matter of fact nervously awaiting some countermove on William's part ever since he committed the outrage.

It was such a very magnificent head-dress that William felt an overpowering sensation of gratitude. It tied his hands. It poisoned his peace of mind. It made him feel obliged to be polite and subservient to Robert, and William hated feeling obliged to be polite and subservient to anyone. He liked to feel free, and untrammelled to carry on that perpetual guerrilla warfare with Robert that lent life some of its necessary zest. The only way of escaping this nauseating sense of obligation was, of course, to bestow upon Robert some magnificent benefit in return—some benefit, in short, commensurate with the feathered head-dress.

William sat in his bedroom gazing at the stupendous gift, torn between ecstasy at its possession, and a hopeless realisation of the impossibility of conferring upon Robert any comparable benefit. He rose, put on his Red Indian suit, tied on the wonderful feather head-band, and, drunk with pride and rapture, swaggered to and fro before his looking-glass. Then he sat down on the floor, and chin in hand, brows drawn into a fierce frown, he thought and thought and thought and thought. What could he give to Robert, what could he do for Robert, to win back his independence of spirit? No light broke in upon the problem. He rose and went to the window. There below him in the garden walked Uncle Frederick with Robert and Flavia upon either side. Uncle Frederick looked very happy. He was gesticulating forcibly as he talked. He was talking about his set of 1923 Esthonia Triangular, over printed and surcharged. Scarce.

Robert walked dejectedly, casting alternate glances of fury at Uncle Frederick and languishment at Flavia. Flavia walked with eyes demurely downcast, occasionally returning Robert's gaze. Emboldened by this, Robert suggested that Uncle Frederick should sit down and rest upon the garden seat and that he and Flavia should have a little game of tennis on the hard court. Uncle Frederick said that he'd love a little game of tennis and that he'd take them both on and beat them both hollow. He went in to change his shoes and dejectedly they followed.

William returned to his seat on the floor and again contorted his freckled countenance into an expression indicative of deep thought. Then suddenly a light shone through it. He rose to his feet and, still wearing his head-dress, performed a dance of victory, snatching up a tooth-brush to wave in lieu of a spear.

He knew now what he was going to do for Robert.

It was the next evening. Flavia had gone out to tea with Mrs. Brown. Robert had very, very moodily gone off for a walk by himself. Uncle Frederick was sitting alone in the dining-room reading the paper.

He was interrupted by the entry of William—William wearing that guileless expression of imbecility that to those who knew him well betokened danger. Uncle Frederick, however, was not among those who knew William well. William sat and looked into the fire in silence, a far-away, wistful expression upon his face. This attracted Uncle Frederick's attention.

"A penny for your thoughts, my little man."

William with an effort concealed his indignation at being thus addressed, and still guilelessly, wistfully replied:

"I was thinking about the wireless Robert's made. It's such a beautiful one."

"Ah!" said Uncle Frederick pleasantly, "I must certainly hear that wireless."

"Would you like to go and hear it now," said William.

"I think that Robert would be so pleased when he came in to know that you'd been listening to his wireless." Again Uncle Frederick was vaguely touched by this.

"Then certainly we must go and listen to it, my little man," he said.

"Will you come now?" said his little man, rising and holding out a grubby hand confidingly.

Uncle Frederick was very, very comfortable, but he could not resist the invitation of that outstretched grubby hand. He rose reluctantly, took it somewhat gingerly and saying heartily:

"Oh, yes, we must certainly hear this wireless. Just for a few minutes, of course. A few minutes, I think, will be enough."

He threw a longing glance at the fire and his newspaper, then yielded to the firm pressure of William's hand and allowed himself to be drawn from the room.

"Here it is," said William. "You just turn this," and William, secure in the knowledge that no programme was going on at the moment, made the reaction handle turn a complete circuit till it was where it had been to start with.

"It will begin in a few minutes now," he said. "Only I've just got to go an' do some lessons. Jus' wait a minute an' it will come. I'm sorry I can't wait."

Uncle Frederick, sitting in front of Robert's wireless which was just in front of the drawn window curtains, waited just a minute or two—waited in fact just long enough for William to run out of the side door round the house, and to put in his head at the open window of the morning room behind the curtain. Then Uncle Frederick's patience was rewarded. A deep bass voice (which those who knew William better might have

"HERE'S ROBERT'S WIRELESS SET, UNCLE FREDERICK," SAID WILLIAM. "YOU JUST TURN THIS, THERE!"

recognised as one of his "disguised" voices) began to speak. It said:

"London callin' the British Isles. There is a ridge of high pressure movin' Eastwards over England, together with a secondary anticyclone deepenin' over Scandinavia.

"There is one S.O.S. Will Mr. Frederick Brown kindly go home at once as his Stamp Collection has been stolen. It——"

But Uncle Frederick could not wait for more. He leapt from his seat, flew up to his bedroom, hastily packed a bag and, hurling an incoherent message at William, rushed forth into the night.

William, looking quite expressionless, explained matters as best he could to his bewildered family on their return.

"Well, he just said he'd had bad news and had to go home. Had he had a telegram? I dunno. P'raps he had. No, I didn't see one. No, he didn't say what sort of bad news. Something about something stolen. Had he been rung up? I dunno. P'raps he had. I wasn't at home in the afternoon. Well, he'd just gone into the morning room to listen to Robert's wireless. I wasn't there with him. I just turned it on for him to listen and then I went out. I *keep tellin'* you I wasn't there with him. He came rushin' out an' said he'd gotter go home. No, why should I know anythin' about it? I *keep tellin'* you. He went into the mornin' room to listen to Robert's wireless and he came rushin' out and went home. Well, how should I know anythin' about it, more'n anyone else?"

Robert's expression throughout the recital had been gradually brightening till it was now a veritable glow. He looked at Flavia.

"Would you care to come out for a little stroll in the garden, Flavia?" he said. "It's quite a nice evening."

And Flavia dimpling demurely murmured: "Yes, I'd love it."

The next morning there arrived a long letter from Uncle Frederick. He told them about the message he'd received by wireless and how he'd been assured by all his friends that no such message had been sent by wireless, and that no such message could have been sent by wireless. They all said that he must have dropped asleep and dreamed it, and that was the explanation that he had finally adopted. He must have dropped into a doze while he sat waiting for the wireless to begin and dreamed it. Anyway, he thought that he'd stay at home now and not return for the remainder of his visit as the incident had made him nervous. Dreams were, he was sure, often sent for a warning and he thought he'd like to be on the spot for the next few months in case there were any thieves about who had their eye on his stamp collection. He was afraid that his two young friends would miss him very much, but he was sure they would forgive him and understand.

* * *

It was evening. All was well. An atmosphere of peace hung over the house. Robert and Flavia had packed a picnic basket and gone off for the day.

William, wearing his new and magnificent headgear, was demonstrating his freshly regained independence of spirit by erecting a cunning arrangement above Robert's bedroom door, whereby when Robert opened it a pillow would drop down and, he hoped, completely envelop Robert's head.

Chapter 8

Williams's Lucky Day

William and the other Outlaws sat in the old barn discussing the latest tragedy that had befallen them. Tragedies, of course, fell thick and fast upon the Outlaws' path through life. They waged ceaseless warfare upon the grown-up world around them and, as was natural, they frequently came off second best. But this was a special tragedy. Not only was it a grown-up victory, but it was a victory that bade fair to make the Outlaws' daily lives a perpetual martyrdom at the hands of their contemporaries.

Usually, the compensating element of a grown-up victory was the fact that it concentrated upon them the sympathy of their associates—a sympathy that not infrequently found tangible form in the shape of bulls-eyes or conkers. But this grown-up victory was a victory that promised to make the lives of the early Christian martyrs beds of roses in comparison with those of the Outlaws.

The way it happened was this.

The headmaster of William's school had a cousin who was a Great Man, and once a year the cousin who was a Great Man came down to the school to address the boys of William's school. He possessed, presumably, gifts of a high and noble order, otherwise he would not have been a Great Man, but whatever those gifts may have been they did not include that of holding the interest of small boys. Only the front two rows could ever hear anything he said and not even the front two rows (carefully chosen by the headmaster for their—misleadingly—intelligent expressions) could understand it.

It might be gathered from this that the annual visit of the Great Man was looked forward to without enthusiasm, but this was not the case, for always at the end of the lecture he turned to the headmaster and asked that the boys might be given a half-holiday the next day, and the headmaster, after simulating first of all intense surprise and then doubt and hesitation, while the rows of small boys watched him in breathless suspense, their eyes nearly dropping out of their heads, finally said that they might. Then someone called for three cheers for the Great Man, and the roof quivered. The Great Man was always much gratified by his reception. He always said afterwards that it was delightful to see young boys taking a deep and intelligent interest in such subjects as Astronomy and Egyptology and Geology, and that the cheers with which they greeted the close of the lecture left him with no doubt at all of their appreciation of it. The school in general went very carefully the day before the lecture because it was known that the headmaster disliked granting the half-holiday and with the meanness of his kind would welcome with hidden joy and triumph any excuse for cancelling it. The Great Man's visit was a nervous strain on the headmaster, and his temper was never at its best just then. To begin with, it was an exhausting and nerve-racking task to discover sufficient boys with intelligent expressions to fill the front rows. Then the other boys had to be graded in dimishing degrees of cleanliness and presentability to the back of the hall which the Great Man, being very short-sighted, could not see, and where the least presentable specimens were massed. The Outlaws were always relegated to the very back row. They found no insult in this, but were, on the contrary, grateful for it. By a slight adjustment of their positions they could hide themselves comfortably from the view of Authority, and give their whole attention to such pursuits as conker battles, the swopping of cigarette-cards, or the "racing" of insects conveyed thither in match-boxes for the purpose. But this year a terrible thing had happened.

The Great Man arrived at the village as usual. As usual he stayed with the headmaster. As usual the Outlaws hid behind the hedge to watch him with interest and curiosity as he passed to and from the headmaster's house, going to the village or returning from it. It was unfortunate that the Great Man happened to be wearing a bowler hat that was undoubtedly too small for him. He may have bought it in a hurry and not realised till he had worn it once or twice how much too small it was, and then with dogged British courage and determination decided to wear it out. He may have been honestly labouring under the delusion that it suited and fitted him. The fact remains that when he emerged from the headmaster's gate into the lane the waiting and watching Outlaws drew deep breaths and ejaculated simultaneously;

"Crumbs! Look at his hat!"

"Don't look like a hat at all," commented Douglas.

"Looks like as if he was carryin' an apple on his head," said Ginger.

"William Tell," said Henry with the modest air of one who, without undue ostentation, has no wish to hide his culture and general information under a bushel. "You know, William Tell. What his father shot an apple off his head without touchin' him."

"An' I bet I could shoot his hat off his head without

touchin' him if I'd got my catapult here," said William, in order to divert the limelight from Henry's intellect to his own physical prowess.

"Bet you couldn't," challenged Ginger.

"Bet I could," said William.

"Bet you couldn't."

"Bet I could."

It was the sort of discussion that can go on for ever. However, when it had gone only about ten minutes, William said with an air of finality:

"Well, I haven't got my catapult, anyway, or else I'd jolly well *show* you."

Ginger unexpectedly produced a catapult.

"Here's mine," he said.

"Well, I haven't got anything to shoot."

Douglas searched in his pocket and produced from beneath the inevitable string, hairy boiled sweets, pen-knife and piece of putty, two or three shrivelled peas.

William was taken aback till he realised that the Great Man had passed out of sight. Then he said, with something of relief: "Well, I can't, can I? Considerin' he's gone!" and added with withering sarcasm, "if you'll kin'ly tell me how to shoot the hat off a person's head what isn't here I'll be very glad to——"

But at that moment the figure of the Great Man was seen returning down the lane. He had only been to the post. The spirit of adventure—that Will-o'-the-wisp that had so often led the Outlaws astray but that they never could resist—entered into them.

"Go on, William," urged Ginger. "Have a shot at his hat an' see if you c'n knock it off. It won't matter. It'll only go 'ping' against his hat and we'll be across the next field before he knows what's happened. He'll never know it was us. Go on, William. Have a shot at his hat."

The figure was abreast of them now on the other side of the hedge.

William, his eyes gleaming with excitement, his face set and stern with determination, raised the catapult and had a shot at the Great Man's hat.

He had been unduly optimistic. He did not shoot the little hat off the Great Man's head as he had boasted he could. Instead he caught the Great Man himself just above his ear. It was, on the whole, not a very bad shot, but William did not stop to point that out to his friends. A dried pea emitted from a catapult can hurt more than those who have never received it have any conception of.

For a minute the Great Man was literally paralysed by the shock. Then he uttered a roar of pain, fury and outraged dignity and started forward, lusting for the blood of his assailant. The dastardly attack had seemed to come from the direction of the hedge. He flung himself in that direction. He could see three boys fleeing over the field and then—clutching desperately at the hedge above him—a fourth boy rolled back into the ditch. The Great Man pounced upon him. It was William, who had caught his foot while scrambling through the hedge, and lost his balance. He bore in his hand the evidence of his guilt in the shape of Ginger's catapult. It was useless for him to deny that he was the perpetrator of the outrage—useless even to plead the analogy of William Tell and the apple.

The Great Man had mastered the first violence of his fury. With a great effort he choked back several expressions which, though forcible, were unsuited for the ears of the young, and fixing William with a stern eye said severely: "I see by your cap that you attend the school at which I am to lecture to-morrow. After this outrage I shall not, of course, ask for the usual half-holiday, and I shall request your headmaster to inform your school-fellows of the reason why no half-holiday is accorded this year."

Then—stern, dignified, an impressive figure were it not for the smallness of his hat, which the shock of William's attack had further knocked slightly crooked—the Great Man passed down the lane.

* * *

William, with pale, set face, returned to his waiting friends.

"*Well!*" he said succinctly, "that's done it. That's jolly well *done* it." Then, savagely, to Ginger: "It's all your fault, taking your silly ole catapult about with you wherever you go an' gettin' people to shoot at other people all over the place. *Now* look what you've done."

"Huh! I like that!" said Ginger with spirit. "I like that. What about *you* falling about in ditches? If *you'd* not gone fallin' about in ditches he'd never've known about it. Huh! A nice Red Indian *you'd* make fallin' about in ditches. An', anyway, you were wrong an' I was right. You *couldn't* shoot his hat off without touchin' his face. I *said* you couldn't."

He ended on a high-pitched note of jeering triumph which the proud spirit of William found intolerable. They hurled themselves upon each other in deadly combat, which was, however, terminated by Henry who enquired with innocent curiosity:

"What did he say, anyway?"

This suddenly reminded William of what the Great Man had said, and his fighting spirit died abruptly.

He sat down on the ground with Ginger on top of him and told them forlornly what the Great Man had said.

On hearing it Ginger's fighting spirit, too, died, and he got off William and sat in the road beside him.

"*Crumbs!*" he said in an awestruck voice of horror.

It was characteristic of the Outlaws that all their mutual recrimination promptly ceased at this news.

This was no mere misfortune. This was tragedy, and a tragedy in which they must all stand together. In the persecution from all ranks of their schoolfellows that would inevitably follow, they must identify themselves with William, their leader; they must share with him the ostracism, and worse than ostracism, that the Great Man's sentence would bring upon them.

"*Crumbs!*" breathed Henry, voicing their feelings, "won't they just be *mad!*"

"I'll tell 'em I did it," said William in a faint voice.

"You didn't do it," said Ginger aggressively. "Whose catapult was it, anyway? An' who dared you to?"

"An' whose pea was it?" put in Douglas with equal indignation.

"I did it, anyway," said William. "It was my fault. I'll tell 'em so."

"It was me just as much as you," said Ginger with spirit.

"It wasn't."

"It was."

"It wasn't."

"It was."

"It wasn't."

This argument, like the previous one, might have developed into a healthy physical contest had not Henry said slowly:

"He can't 've told *him* yet 'cause *he's* gone up to London to choose prizes an' I heard someone say he wun't be back till the last train to-night."

There was a silence. Through four grimy, freckled, disconsolate faces shone four sudden gleams of hope.

"P'raps if you told him you were sorry an' ask him not to——" suggested Douglas.

William leapt to his feet with alacrity.

"Come on," he said tersely and followed by his faithful band made his way across the field through the hedge and down the lane that led to the headmaster's house.

He performed an imperious and very lengthy tattoo on the knocker—a tattoo meant to be indicative of the strength and durability of his repentance.

A pretty housemaid appeared.

She saw one small and very dirty boy on the doorstep and three other small and very dirty boys hanging over the gate. She eyed them with disfavour. She disliked small and dirty boys.

"We're not deaf," she said haughtily.

"Aren't you?" said William with polite interest. "I'm not either. But I've gotter naunt what's so deaf that——"

"What do you want?" she snapped.

William, pulled up in this pleasant chat with the pretty housemaid, remembered what he wanted and said gloomily: "I want to speak to the man what's staying with the headmaster."

"What's your name?"

"William Brown."

"Well, stay there, and I'll ask him."

"All right," said William preparing to enter.

She pushed him back.

"I'm not having them boots in my hall," she said with passionate indignation, and went in, closing the door upon him.

William looked down at his boots with a puzzled frown and then called anxiously to his friends over the gate:

"There's nothing wrong with my boots, is there?"

They looked at William's boots, large, familiar, mud-encrusted.

"No," they said, "they're quite all right."

"What's she talkin' about, then?" said William.

"P'raps she means they're *muddy*," suggested Douglas tentatively.

"Well, that's what boots are *for*, i'n't it?" said William sternly.

Just then the housemaid returned and opened the door.

"He says if you're the boy who's just shot a catapult at him, certainly not."

It was quite obvious from William's expression that he *was* the boy.

"Well, what I wanted to say was that——"

Slowly but very firmly she was closing the door upon him. William planted one of his boots in the track of the closing door.

"Look here!" he said desperately, "tell him he can shoot a catapult at me. I don't mind. Look here. Tell him I'll put an apple on my head, an' he can——"

Again the housemaid indignantly pushed him back.

"Look at my *step!*" she said fiercely as she closed the door. "*You* and your *boots!*"

The door was quite closed now.

William opened the flap of the letter-box with his hand and said hoarsely:

"Tell him that it was all because of his hat. Say that——"

But she'd disappeared and it was obvious that she didn't intend to return.

He rejoined his friends at the gate.

" 'S no good," he said dejectedly. "She won't even listen to me. Jus' keeps on talkin' about my boots.

WILLIAM PLANTED HIS FOOT IN THE TRACK OF THE CLOSING DOOR. "LOOK HERE!" HE SAID DESPERATELY. "TELL HIM HE CAN SHOOT A CATAPULT AT ME. I DON'T MIND!"

They're jus' the same as anyone else's boots, as far as I can see. Anyway, what're we goin' to do now?"

"Let's find out what he's doin' to-night," said Ginger. "If he's goin' anywhere you might meet him on the way an' see if he'll listen to you."

"Yes," said William, "that's a jolly good idea, but—how're we goin' to find out what he's doin' to-night?"

"It's after tea-time," announced Henry rather pathetically. (Henry hated missing his meals.) "I votes we go home to tea now and then come back an' talk it over some more."

"I shouldn't be surprised if it's goin' to be rather hard," said William still dejectedly, "findin' out what he's goin' to do to-night."

But it turned out to be quite simple.

While Douglas was having tea he heard his father say to his mother that he'd heard that the headmaster's cousin was going to dine with the Carroways, as the headmaster had gone to London on business and wasn't coming back till the last train.

Douglas joyfully took this news back to the meeting of the Outlaws.

They gave him a hearty cheer and William began to look as if the whole thing was now settled.

"*That's* all right," he said. "Now I'll go 'n' stay by the front gate of the Carroway house till he comes along and then I'll plead with him."

They looked at him rather doubtfully. Somehow they couldn't visualise William pleading. William defying, William commanding, were familiar figures, but they had never yet seen William pleading.

"We'll come along with you," said Ginger, "an' help you."

"All right," said William cheerfully. "We'll all plead.

It oughter melt him all right, *four* people pleadin'. What time ought we to be there?"

"I 'spect they have dinner at half-past seven," said Ginger.

"Let's be there at quarter past six so's to be quite sure not to miss him."

* * *

They reached the Carroways' at a quarter past six and took up their posts by the gate. So far, so good. All would, in fact, have gone splendidly had not a circus happened to be in the act of unloading itself in the field next to the Carroways' house. The Outlaws caught a glimpse of tents, vans, cages. They heard the sound of a muffled roar, they distinctly saw an elephant. It was more than flesh and blood could stand.

"Well," said William carelessly, "we've got here too early an' it's no good wastin' time hangin' about. Let's jus' go'n wait in the field jus' for five minutes or so. That can't do any harm."

Douglas, who was of a cautious disposition, demurred, but his protests were half-hearted and already the others were through the hedge and making their way to the little crowd that surrounded the caravans and cages. It was beyond their wildest dreams. There was a lion. There was a tiger. There was an elephant. There was a bear. There were several monkeys. They saw a monkey bite a piece out of someone's trousers. William laughed at this so much that they thought he was going to be sick. The bear sat on its hind legs and flapped its arms. The lion roared. The elephant took someone's hat off. The whole thing was beyond description.

The Outlaws wandered about, getting in everyone's way, putting their noses through the bars of every cage, miraculously escaping sudden death at every turn. It was when William thought that they must have been there nearly five minutes that they asked the time and found that it was twenty past seven. They had been there over an hour.

"*Crumbs!*" they ejaculated in dismay, and William said slowly:

"Seems impossible to me. P'raps," with sudden hope, "their clocks are wrong."

But their clocks weren't wrong. They asked four or five other men and were impatiently given the same reply.

Aghast, they wandered back to the gate where they had meant to accost the Great Man, but they realised that it was no use waiting there now. He would certainly have arrived by now.

"Let's go up the drive," said Ginger, "an' see if we c'n see him."

They crept up the drive. Dusk was falling quickly and the downstairs rooms were lit up. The drawing-room curtains were not drawn and the Outlaws were rewarded by the sight of the Great Man standing on the hearthrug talking to Mr. and Mrs. Carroway.

They stared at him forlornly from the bushes.

"*Well!*" moaned William, "of all the *rotten* luck!"

Then they discussed the crisis in hoarse whispers. It would be impossible, of course, to wait till he came home and by to-morrow he would have seen and reported matters to the headmaster. Anyone less determined than the Outlaws would have abandoned the project and gone home. But not the Outlaws.

"Let's go round to the other side of the house," said William, "an' have a look at the dining-room. We might get a chance to whisper to him through the window or somethin'."

This was felt to be unduly optimistic, but the suggestion appealed to the Outlaws' spirit of adventure and they followed William round to the side of the house.

The dining-room window was open but the curtains were drawn. The curtains, however, did not quite meet at the top and William said that by climbing on to the roof of the summer-house he thought he could see into the room.

Using Ginger and Douglas as a step ladder, he hoisted himself up on to the roof of the summer-house. It was now so dark that he could not see the Outlaws down among the bushes.

"I can't see into the room yet," he whispered, "but," he added optimistically, "I bet if I stand on tiptoe——"

At this point the Outlaws became conscious of some sort of a commotion, of the sound of many excited voices. Then a man with a lighted lantern began to make what was obviously a tour of inspection of the garden.

William crouched down upon his summer-house and the others crouched down among the bushes.

The man with the lighted lantern passed, muttering to himself.

* * *

The Great Man stood in the drawing-room talking to Mr. and Mrs. Carroway and to Mrs. Carroway's companion, Miss Seed.

It was, of course, unfortunate that Mrs. Carroway's companion was called Miss Seed, and had there been any other suitable applicant for the post Mrs. Carroway would certainly not have chosen Miss Seed. However, there hadn't been, so both of them made the best of the situation and had brought to a fine art the capacity of looking quite unconscious when their names were pronounced together.

The Great Man was talking. The Great Man was, as a matter of fact, never completely happy unless he was talking, and he had been pleased to find that he was the only guest because he so often found that other guests liked to talk as well, and that completely spoilt the evening for him. He was, however, rather annoyed when Mrs. Carroway was called out to someone at the front door in the middle of his very brilliant summary of the political situation. He cleared his throat in an annoyed fashion, frowned, and stood in silence watching the door for her return. He didn't consider Mr. Carroway alone worth addressing, and Miss Seed had gone out to see to the dinner, because Mrs. Carroway was, as usual, without maids and one of the reasons why Mrs. Carroway had chosen Miss Seed as a companion, despite her name, was that she did not mind seeing to dinners in the intervals of companioning Mrs. Carroway. After a few minutes Mrs. Carroway returned.

"When I say that this Government has missed some of its finest opportunities," he began at once, "I refer of course——"

But Mrs. Carroway didn't wait to hear to what he referred. She didn't care at all what opportunities the Government had missed.

"What *shall* we do?" she burst out hysterically. "Here's a man to say that a lion has escaped from the circus and they think it may be in our back garden, because there's only a fence between our back garden and the field where the circus is. Oh, what *shall* we do? We shall all be eaten alive."

The Great Man cleared his throat and took command of the situation.

"Send the man round the garden to search," he said, "and we will meantime remain perfectly calm and lock up all the doors and windows. Be brave, Mrs. Carroway, and trust yourself to my protection. I will see that all the doors and windows are securely fastened. Courage! Remember we are English men and, ahem, English women, and must show no fear. Lock and bolt the front door at once and shout through the letter-box to the man to make a thorough search of the garden."

This was done. The man seemed slightly peeved and went off alone muttering.

The Great Man then made a tour of the house, closing every door and window firmly. Finally, he collected Mr. and Mrs. Carroway and Miss Seed into the drawing-room where he locked the shutters and moved the grand piano across the door.

"Let courage and fortitude be our motto," he said. "Let us now meet danger calmly."

No one listened to him. Miss Seed was tending Mrs. Carroway who was in hysterics and was hoping that she'd soon be sufficiently recovered to allow her to have them in her turn, and Mr. Carroway was trying to get under the sofa.

The Great Man, therefore, had no one to address but his own reflection in the full-length mirror. So he addressed it spiritedly.

"England expects——" he began. At this moment there came a loud rat-tat-tat at the knocker. Mrs. Carroway, who was just coming out of hysterics, went into them again, and Mr. Carroway put his head out of the sofa to say reassuringly: "Don't be alarmed, dearest. It can't be the lion. The lion couldn't reach up to the knocker."

Then someone pushed open the letter-box and the voice of the man with the lantern called: "He ain't in your garden, mister. I've been all over your garden," and added sarcastically: "You can come out from hunder the sofa. 'E won't 'urt you."

MR. CARROWAY CRAWLED OUT FROM UNDER THE SOFA.
"A NICE THING!" HE SAID. "A NICE THING, THIS!"

"What a very impertinent man," said Mr. Carroway. "I shall report him to the manager of his firm."

The Great Man began to unbarricade the door.

"We may all justly pride ourselves," he said, "upon the dauntless courage we have displayed in face of this crisis."

"I'm so hungry," said Miss Seed pathetically.

"Hungry?" said Mrs. Carroway. "I'm *past* hunger. I

THE GREAT MAN BEGAN TO UNBARRICADE THE DOOR. "WE MAY ALL JUSTLY PRIDE OURSELVES," HE SAID, "UPON OUR DAUNTLESS COURAGE!"

shall never, never, *never* be able to describe to you what I've suffered during these last few minutes."

Mr. Carroway looked rather relieved at the information.

They went into the dining-room and took their seats. Miss Seed brought in the dinner, and the Great Man returned to the opportunities the Government had missed.

"I still feel faint," said Mrs. Carroway, unwilling to share the limelight with the government or anyone else. "I still feel most faint. I always do after any nervous shock."

Her husband went to the window and drew back the curtains and opened the window.

"I—I don't know that I'd do that," said Mrs. Carroway, gazing fearfully out into the dark garden. "One can't be *quite* sure—I mean——"

At that moment came the sound of a heavy body crashing through the undergrowth. With a wild scream Mrs. Carroway rose and fled from the room.

"Quick," she panted, "out of the front door and across to the Vicarage for refuge. The creature is gathering for a spring. This house is unsafe——"

She was half-way down the front drive by this time, followed closely by the others. The Great Man, being far from nimble on his feet, panted along at the end, gasping, "Courage, friends . . . let courage be our motto."

The house was left empty and silent.

* * *

The sound of the heavy crashing through the undergrowth had of course been William leaping down from the roof of the shed to join his companions below, losing his balance just as he leapt, and falling among the laurel bushes.

He sat up, rubbing his head and ejecting laurel leaves from his mouth. Then: "I say, what's all the fuss about?" he whispered. "I thought I heard someone scream."

"So'd I," said the Outlaws mystified.

"What was that man goin' round with a lantern for?" whispered William.

"I d'no," said the Outlaws, still more mystified.

"Well," said William, abandoning the mystery for the moment, "let's go an' see if we can see what they're doing' now. Someone's drawn the curtains."

They crept up through the bushes to the open dining-room window. To their amazement they saw a brightly lit room, a table laid for four, steaming dishes upon it, and chairs drawn up in position—all completely empty.

"Crumbs!" said William in amazement, "that's queer."

The Outlaws gazed in silence at the astounding sight till Ginger said weakly:

"Where've they all *gone* to?"

"P'raps they're in the other room," suggested Douglas.

They crept round to the drawing-room window. The drawing-room was empty.

"P'raps—p'raps," said Henry without conviction, "they're all in the kitchen."

They crept round to the kitchen. The kitchen was empty. They looked at the upstairs windows. They were all in darkness.

William scratched his head and frowned.

" 'S very mysterious," he commented.

Then they returned to the dining-room. It was still empty. The steaming dishes were still upon the table. An odour was wafted out to the waiting Outlaws—an odour so succulent that it was impossible to resist it. It was William who first swung himself over the low window sill of the open window into the room. The others followed. They stood in silence and gazed at the steaming dishes on the table, the four places, the four chairs.

"Seems," said Ginger dreamily, "seems sort of like a fairy-tale—like a sort of Arabian Nights story."

"Well," said William slowly, "it cert'nly seems sort of *meant*."

"I read a tale once like this," said Douglas, "and they sat down at the table and invisible hands waited on them."

"Let's try," said William suddenly, taking his seat at the head of the table, "let's try if invisible hands'll wait on us."

They needed no encouragement. They all took their seats with alacrity. In fairness to whatever invisible hands might have waited upon the Outlaws, it must be admitted that they did not get much chance. The Outlaws began immediately to wait upon themselves with visible and very grimy hands. Each had a suspicion that at any minute the feast might be interrupted. None of them really had much faith in the Arabian Nights idea. Under the cover in front of William was a roast chicken. The dishes contained bread sauce, gravy, potatoes and cauliflower. William dismembered the chicken ruthlessly and with a fine disregard for anatomy, and they helped themselves from the various dishes. It was a glorious meal. There was in the room complete silence, broken only by the sounds of the Outlaws endeavouring to put away as much of this gorgeous repast as they could before the dream should fade into reality, and some grown-up confront them, demanding explanation. They did not draw breath till every dish was bare and then, flushed and panting, they sat back and

William said meditatively: "Wonder what they were goin' to have after this?"

Douglas suggested giving the invisible hands a chance, but the suggestion was not popular and Henry, catching sight of a hatch in the wall, went to investigate. The hatch slid up and on the ledge just inside was waiting a magnificent cream edifice and a little pile of four plates. Four gasps of ecstasy went up. Again there was silence, broken only by the sounds of the Outlaws working hard against time. At last that dish, too, was empty. There was a barrel of biscuits and a pile of fruit on the sideboard, but the capacity even of the Outlaws was exhausted.

"I feel I wouldn't want to eat another thing for hundreds and hundreds of years," said Henry blissfully.

"Seems about time we woke up now," said Douglas.

But to William, who lived ever in the present, the feast, though the most gorgeous of its kind he had ever known, was already a thing of the past, and he was concentrating his whole attention on the problem of the present.

"I wonder what's *happened* to 'em?" he said. "I wonder where they *are*."

"Looks like the thing old Markie was tellin' us about in school yesterday," said Henry, "a place where a volcano went off suddenly, an' killed all the people and left their houses an' furniture an' things an' you can see it to-day. It's called Pomples or somethin' like that."

This information as emanating from Authority and savouring of swank was rightly ignored.

"P'raps they've all died suddenly of the plague or something," suggested Douglas cheerfully.

But the best suggestion came from Ginger.

"I guess someone's murdered them an' hid all their dead bodies upstairs. I bet if we go upstairs we'll find all their dead bodies hid there."

Much inspirited at this prospect the Outlaws swarmed upstairs and concluded a thorough search of the premises. The search was disappointing.

"Not many dead bodies," said William rather bitterly.

Ginger, feeling that his prestige had suffered from his failure to prove his theory, looked about him and with a yell of glee, said:

"No, but look! There's a trap-door up there and I bet we could get out on to the roof from it."

The Outlaws completely forgot both feast and dead bodies in the thrill of the trap-door by which you could get out on to the roof.

"Who'll try it first?" said William.

"Bags me. I saw it first," said Ginger.

He climbed on to the balusters, leapt at the trap-door, caught it by a miracle, and swung himself up. It was a spectacle guaranteed to give any mother nervous breakdowns for months.

"Does it go out on to the roof?" called the Outlaws, breathless with suspense.

Faint but ecstatic came back Ginger's voice:

"Yes, it does. It's scrummy. Right on the edge of the roof. I can see right down into the garden. I can——"

"Shut up," hissed William, "someone's coming."

* * *

Downstairs Mr. and Mrs. Carroway, Miss Seed and the Great Man entered the hall and hastily shut and locked the front door.

They had gone to the Vicarage and stayed there for an hour. To the Vicar and his wife it had seemed much more than an hour because Mrs. Carroway was acquiring a fatal facility in hysterics and was apparently beginning to count every moment wasted that was not devoted to them.

Finally the Vicar rang up the police, learnt that the missing lion had been seen going down the road at the other end of the village, and politely but firmly insisted on his guests departing homewards. He was beginning to fear the effect of Mrs. Carroway's hysterics upon his wife. No woman likes being put so completely in the shade as Mrs. Carroway's hysterics put the Vicar's wife, and he had noticed that she was beginning to watch the various stages of the attacks with an interest that suggested to him that she was storing them up for future use.

"Nothing," wailed Mrs. Carroway, "*nothing* will induce me to leave this house again to-night. What I have suffered during that terrible walk from the Vicarage, hearing and seeing lions at every step, no one will ever understand. *No* one. If I talked all night I couldn't make you understand."

"I'm sure you couldn't, dear," said her husband hastily.

"I—er—I suppose the house *is* safe," said the Great Man uneasily. "I—er—I cannot help remembering that we left the—er—the dining-room window open and that the—er—the place from which the—er—the beast escaped was—er—just over the fence."

"Miss Seed," said Mrs. Carroway faintly, "go and see whether there are any traces of it in the dining-room. The food, you remember, was left on the table. If that has been tampered with——"

Miss Seed sidled cautiously to the dining-room and peeped in. Then she gave a wild scream.

"It's been here," she panted. "It's been here. It's been here. It's eaten up everything. It must be in the house—NOW!"

Miss Seed, of course, was overwrought, or she would have stopped to take into consideration the fact that a lion does not eat out of a plate with knives and forks and spoons and that even if it did one lion would not have used four of each.

"It must be in the house NOW!" she repeated desperately.

There was a sudden silence—a silence of paralysed horror. Through this silence came the sound of a heavy crash upstairs, followed by a snarl of rage.

In less time than it takes to tell the hall was empty.

Mrs. Carroway had locked herself into the conservatory.

Miss Seed was under the drawing-room sofa.

Mr. Carroway was on the drawing-room mantel piece.

The Great Man was in the rug box in the hall.

The heavy crash had been Ginger overbalancing and falling back through the trap-door upon William in his over anxiety to find out what was going on. The snarl of rage was William's involuntary reaction to the sudden descent of Ginger's solid form upon him.

The Outlaws, aghast at the noise they had made, froze into a petrified silence.

The four grown-ups, in their hiding-places downstairs, also froze in a petrified silence.

Complete silence reigned throughout the house.

The minutes passed slowly by—one minute, two minutes, three minutes, five minutes. Of the eight people in the house no one spoke, no one moved, no one breathed.

At last William whispered: "They must've gone out again."

"I din't hear the door," hissed Ginger.

"I'm goin' to see," said William.

He peeped cautiously over the balusters. The hall was

empty. The only sound was the solemn ticking of the grandfather clock.

"I b'lieve they *have* gone out again," whispered William. "I'm goin' down. Seems to me they're all potty."

He took off his shoes, crept silently down the stairs to the empty, silent hall and stood there irresolute.

Then he thought he heard a movement in a chest near the clock. He approached it and listened. Heavy, raucous breathing came from inside. He raised the lid. As he did so there came from it a high-pitched scream of terror. The open lid revealed the Great Man. The high-pitched scream of terror had come from the Great Man. William stared at him in blank amazement.

The Great Man, instead of seeing the fanged, tawny face he had expected when the chest lid began slowly to open, met the astonished gaze of the boy who had shot at him with a catapult that morning.

They stared at each other in silence. Then a thoughtful expression came over the face of the Great Man.

"Er—was it you who made that noise upstairs?" he said.

"Yes," said William. "Ginger fell on me. I bet you'd've made a noise if Ginger'd fell on you."

The expression of the Great Man became yet more thoughtful.

"And the—er—the dinner——?" he said, still reclining in the rug box.

"Yes," admitted William, "it—it seemed sort of *meant*."

Slowly, stiffly, the Great Man climbed out of the rug box. It had been a very tight fit.

Just then the telephone bell rang, and the Great Man went to answer it. He was glad of the diversion. He was remembering more and more clearly the high-pitched

WILLIAM AND THE GREAT MAN STARED BLANKLY AT EACH OTHER. "ER—WAS IT YOU WHO MADE THAT NOISE UPSTAIRS?" THE GREAT MAN ASKED.

cry of terror he had uttered as the chest opened. He was wondering what explanation he could give this boy of that and of his presence in the rug box.

The telephone call was from the police. The lion had been found. The rumour that it had been seen at the other end of the village had proved to be incorrect. On escaping from its cage it had wandered into the further field and gone to sleep in the shelter of a hayrick. It had just been discovered, roused and taken back to its cage.

* * *

Within a few minutes Miss Seed was putting Mrs. Carroway to bed, Mr. Carroway was trying to mend the more valuable of the ornaments he had displaced from the mantelpiece in his hurried ascent, and the Great Man had called William aside. The Great Man was aware that this was a situation requiring delicate handling. He had tried to think of some dignified explanation of his presence in the rug box and of that unfortunate scream, and not one had occurred to him. He had decided, therefore, not to attempt any. Instead he assumed his most genial expression and said:

"I believe, my boy, that you—er—are the boy who accidentally—er—hit me with some missile this morning."

"Yes," said William simply, "a pea."

"I have no doubt at all," said the Great Man, "that it was—er—an accident, and—ahem—I do not after all intend to mention the matter to your headmaster."

"Thank you," said William, but without much enthusiasm. William knew when he held the reins of a situation in his hand.

The Great Man continued: "No need for you—ahem—for you to mention to anyone what has occurred here to-night."

William said nothing. His face was drained of expression. His eye was blank.

"I will, of course," went on the Great Man hastily, "I will-ahem—of course ask for the usual half-holiday from your headmaster."

William turned upon the Great Man his expressionless face and his blank eye and said suavely:

"Why not ask for two, sir?"

The Great Man swallowed and cleared his throat. Then, with a more or less convincing attempt at heartiness, he said: "Certainly, my boy. Certainly. A very good idea. I'll ask for two. And with regard to what happened here to-night——"

The Great Man was uncomfortably aware that the story of what had happened there that night as told by this boy might take some living down.

But William's face was still expressionless, his eye still blank.

"You hidin' in that box to give me a fright?" he said carelessly. "Oh, no! Why, I've nearly forgot that already." His blank, unblinking eye was fixed upon the Great Man. "I bet that after two half-holidays I'll have forgot it altogether."

* * *

The Great Man brought out the request for two half-holidays with something of an effort. The headmaster wasn't prepared for it and was taken aback. However, he didn't want to offend the Great Man, so after a brief inward struggle he promised the two half-holidays.

Frenzied cheers rent the air.

At the back of the hall, in the back row, sat William nonchalantly manufacturing a blotting-paper dart, wholly unmoved apparently by the glorious news.

"Din't you hear?" yelled a frenzied neighbour, "din't you *hear? Two* half-holidays."

"Yes, I heard all right," said William carelessly.

And, making careful aim, threw his dart at Ginger.

Chapter 9

A Little Adventure

William and Ginger walked slowly down the village street. They were discussing with much animation some burglaries that had lately taken place in the village.

"Robert says," said William, "that *he* b'lieves that it's not ordin'ry robbers at all an' that *he* b'lieves that it's people livin' in the place, people what *seem* all right an' go about doin' shoppin' an' going' to church an' going out to tea same as orn'ery people. He's been readin' a book where that happened—someone what was churchwarden in the daytime an' went out stealin' at night. Robert says that he's goin' to try to find out who it is."

"I bet I know why he wants to find out who it is," said Ginger with a note of bitterness in his voice.

"Why?" challenged William.

" 'Cause of that Miss Bellairs," said Ginger.

Miss Bellairs was Robert's latest inamorata. Robert's love affairs were of such a kaleidoscopic nature that William had long ago ceased to trouble to keep up with them but not even William had been able quite to ignore the affair with Miss Bellairs. Miss Bellairs was an (in William's eye) elderly woman of about twenty who had come to stay in the village with her aunt. Her aunt had a son who was the object of Robert's deadly jealousy. So much William knew, and he knew it only because it was impossible to live in the same house as Robert and not know it. He took no interest in it. He did not know or care where the girl's aunt lived or what she was called or anything else about the matter whatsoever. He was annoyed at Ginger's remark, suspecting a hidden insult in it.

"What d'you know about *that?*" he said aggressively.

"I know 'cause Hector's potty on her, too," said Ginger dejectedly.

Hector was Ginger's elder brother. He was (in the Outlaw's eyes) as lacking in sanity and consideration for his youngers as are all elder brothers.

William's aggressiveness vanished. He felt drawn to Ginger by a common bond of misfortune and shame.

"Can't make out what makes 'em act like that about her," he said with fierce exasperation in his voice. "I've seen her an' she looks perfectly orn'ery to me."

"Me, too," agreed Ginger with heartfelt emphasis, and added scornfully. "*Girls!* I'm jolly well not going' to *speak* to a girl 'cept what you have to all my life."

"Same here," agreed William.

This agreement seemed to form a yet closer bond between them and, each feeling cheered and invigorated by the knowledge that the world held at least one person of intelligence besides himself, they returned to the subject of the burglaries. They discussed burglaries in general and the present village burglaries in particular. They discussed burglary as a career and finally decided that it was less exciting than that of piracy though more exciting than that of engine driver—careers to which they had always inclined.

They had been walking aimlessly along the road without noticing particularly where they were going, and they discovered suddenly that they were passing Ginger's aunt's house.

"Let's see if we can see her parrot," said Ginger.

"It'll probably be in the front room."

They crept cautiously up to the window. Ginger's aunt was what is known as "house proud" and Ginger—leaver of muddy boot marks and sticky finger marks, breaker of nearly everything he touched—knew that he was not a welcome visitor to her house. He was not at all sensitive to shades of manner, but she had left him in no doubt at all on that subject.

Therefore he crept furtively up to her front window in order to enjoy the intriguing spectacle of his aunt's parrot hopping up and down upon its perch and uttering malicious chuckles.

"I bet she's out," said Ginger. "She always goes out shopping in the mornings. Let's open the window an' listen to it."

They opened the window cautiously and put their heads inside. The parrot began to jump up and down on his perch still more excitedly when he saw them.

"Hello, Polly!" said William encouragingly.

"Oh, shut up," said the parrot.

This delighted his visitors.

"Go on, Polly," encouraged Ginger. "Go on! Say something else."

"Get out, you old fool," said the parrot with a snigger.

"Jolly good, isn't it?" said Ginger proudly. "And it's quite tame. It comes out an' sits on your finger. My aunt lets me take it out and hold it. At least," he corrected himself, "she used to before that last vase got broke. How could I know," he added bitterly, "that a vase would fall off the hall table on to the floor an' get broke simply with me comin' downstairs?"

William made a vague sound suggestive of sympathy but he was not really interested in the disastrous reverberations of Ginger's footfall. He was interested in the parrot.

"I bet it doesn't jus' sit quietly on *your* finger," he said. "It knows *her* finger, of course, but I bet if you took it out it wouldn't sit quiet on yours."

"It would," affirmed Ginger aggressively.

"Easy to say that," said William, "when you know that you can't try."

"I *can* try," said Ginger. "She's out shoppin', anyway. She always is in the morning. I bet you *anythin'* it'll sit quiet on my finger. It won't take a *second.* Let's jus' get in an' see."

He raised the window and with a cautious glance around the room entered. William followed. The parrot gave its most vulgar snigger and said: "Oh, shut up." It was certainly an attractive bird. . . .

With another hasty glance round Ginger opened the catch of the cage and put out his finger ready for the bird to alight upon.

The bird said: "Get out, you old fool," and hopped obligingly on to Ginger's ginger.

"*There!*" said Ginger proudly standing with his arm outstretched. "There! What did I *tell* you?"

For a second he stood like that with an indescribable swagger in his pose, holding out the bird at arm's length. For a second only. At the end of a second the bird suddenly spread its wings and without any warning at all flew straight out of the window. The swagger dropped incontinently from Ginger's pose. He gazed at the open window, his freckled face pale, his mouth open.

"*Crumbs!*" he gasped.

"*Crumbs!*" echoed William.

Then both of them dived simultaneously through the window into the garden.

There they gazed around them. The parrot was sitting quite calmly on a low bush in the next-door neighbour's garden.

The two Outlaws crept up to the fence and climbing over it, approached the parrot. The parrot awaited their approach, chuckling his most malicious chuckle. He let them come up quite close to him. He waited till Ginger had put out a hand to grab him, and then with a combination of his malicious chuckle and his vulgar snigger he flew off from under Ginger's very hand through the open window into the next door house.

"*Crumbs!*" said Ginger again in a tone of helpless horror.

William crept cautiously up to the window.

"I can see him," he whispered, "he's sittin' on the piano."

"Is there anyone in the room?" whispered Ginger from behind the laurel bush where he had taken cover.

"No. No one. Just a lot of chairs. I'll go in an' fetch him. I'll jus' get in at this window an' fetch him. I'll——"

He was cautiously pushing up the window.

"I'll come too," volunteered Ginger somewhat dispiritedly. Mental visions of his aunt when she discovered that her pet was missing were beginning to haunt him.

"No. Best let only one go alone," said William, "then if anything happens to me you'll be safe to go on lookin' for it."

William's spirits were rising at the prospects of an adventure.

He swung himself over the sill and found himself in a small drawing-room. It was full of chairs arranged in rows as if for a meeting and there was a table at one end.

"Oh, shut up," said the parrot excitedly from the piano.

William began to stalk his prey in his best Red Indian fashion. It waited till his hand was nearly on him then, chuckling, flew to the mantelpiece.

"Polly, Polly," whispered William in fierce, hoarse coaxing as he approached the mantelpiece.

"Get out, you old fool," said the parrot who seemed to be thoroughly enjoying himself. He let William think that he was really going to get him this time, then with another chuckle spread his wings and flew off again. This time he circled round and round the room and finally disappeared behind a cabinet that stood across a corner of the room, having a fair-sized recess between it and the wall.

William was just pursuing it to this retreat when the door opened and a tall, stern-looking woman wearing pince-nez and a high collar entered the room. She looked at William in surprise and disapproval.

"You mustn't come into a house like this without knocking at the door," she said. "If you've come to the meeting you should have knocked at the door properly and, anyway, the meeting doesn't begin till half-past. Have you come to the meeting?"

William hesitated. If he told her that he had come to catch Ginger's aunt's escaped parrot then there was no doubt at all that Ginger's aunt would hear of the escapade from her neighbour and it was of vital importance to Ginger's peace of mind and body that the parrot should be caught and returned to its cage without Ginger's aunt having known of its escape. It seemed better therefore on the whole to have come to the meeting.

"Yes," he said, assuming his blankest expression.

Then another lady very like the first one came in and stared at William.

"Who is this boy and what's he doing here?" she said to the first lady.

"He says he's come to the meeting," said the first lady helplessly.

"But, my *dear!*" said the second lady, "we don't want people like *that* at the meeting. A rough-looking boy like *that!*"

The first lady grew yet more helpless.

"But we've advertised it as a public meeting," she said. "We can't turn people away, I mean—*well* we *can't*. I don't think it would be legal," she ended vaguely.

"But what does he *want* to come to the meeting for?" said the second lady. "And a quarter of an hour too early, too."

"I suppose he's interested in Total Abstinence," said the first lady doubtfully. "I suppose there's no reason why he shouldn't be." She turned to William. "Are you interested in Total Abstinence?"

"Yes," said William without a second's hesitation and looking blanker than ever.

Both ladies stared at him and looked very much perplexed.

Then a man with crossed eyes behind huge horn-rimmed spectacles and carrying a sheaf of papers entered and said briskly:

"Is everything ready?"

The first lady pointed to William.

"This boy says he's interested in Total Abstinence and wants to come to the meeting," she said.

William turned a sphinx-like face to the man.

The man subjected William to a lengthy inspection. William met it unblinkingly. The lengthy inspection did not seem to reassure the young man at all. He said reluctantly:

"Well, I suppose we can't turn him out if he wants to come. I mean we've *advertised* it as a public meeting——"

"Just what I said," said the first lady.

"But any monkey tricks from you, my boy——" said the man threateningly.

"*Me!*" said William, his sphinx-like look changing to one of righteous indignation. "*Me!*" He seemed hardly able to believe his ears.

"All right," said the man irritably. "Go and sit down somewhere at the back. People will be coming in in a minute."

William chose a seat just in front of the cabinet behind which the parrot had taken refuge. The parrot was preserving a strange silence. William made violent efforts to see it from his chair till the second lady said:

"Do sit still there, boy! You make me feel quite giddy fidgeting about like that."

So William sat (comparatively) still, wondering how he could entice the parrot from behind the cabinet and make his departure with it unobserved. The parrot's silence puzzled him. Was it merely resting after the excitement of its flight or was it planning some outrageous piece of devilry? People were beginning to arrive now. They all threw glances at William, curious and in most cases disapproving. William's whole energy was now taken up in meeting their glances with his blankest stare.

Evidently one lady (who presumably knew him) was objecting to his presence because he heard the first lady saying helplessly:

"Well, I don't see how we *can* turn him out. He said that he wanted to come to the meeting because he was interested in Total Abstinence . . . and he isn't *doing* anything we can turn him out for."

Fortunately the chair William occupied stood by itself next to the cabinet. Just in front of him was the last row of chairs. The chairs were all full now and the meeting was beginning. He was craning his neck round to see what had happened to the parrot. There was still no sound from behind the cabinet. . . . He began to think that it must have gone to sleep. . . .

The cross-eyed man was speaking. "It gives me great pleasure to introduce to you our speaker, Miss Rubina Thomasina Fawshaw. Her name is well known, of course, to all of us——"

It was at this point that the parrot behind the cabinet suddenly ejaculated.

"Oh, shut up!"

The meeting wheeled round to gaze at William open-mouthed with horror and indignation. William with a great effort maintained his sphinx-like expression and stared fixedly in front of him, trying to look as if he were in a brown study and had not heard the interruption.

The man was fortunately rather deaf. After looking about him vaguely for some minutes he continued. With a last stern and threatening glance at William the audience turned round again to listen.

"She is a splendid and well-known worker in this noble cause. She has for the last six weeks been travelling in America, and she has there studied the question of Prohibition in all its aspects——"

"Get out, you old fool!"

They all swung round again. It couldn't have come from anyone but William. William was making a supreme and quite unconvincing attempt to look innocent. He was staring in front of him with a set, fixed stare and a purple face. The man with the squint had heard now. Fixing one furious eye on William and the other out of the window he said:

"One more such interruption from you, my boy, and out you go."

The unhappy William made a vague sound in his throat suggestive of innocence and surprise and apology

"GET OUT, YOU OLD FOOL!" SAID A VOICE. WILLIAM WAS STARING IN FRONT OF HIM WITH A SET, FIXED STARE.

and continued to stare fixedly in front of him. After another short silence the cross-eyed man continued his speech. The audience, pausing only to throw final vitriolic glances at William, turned round again to listen.

"I personally," went on the cross-eyed man, "have known Miss Fawshaw for a good many years——"

"ONE MORE INTERRUPTION FROM YOU, MY BOY," SAID THE MAN WITH THE SPECTACLES, "AND OUT YOU GO!"

There was no mistaking it. It was a vulgar snigger coming from the back of the room where William sat.

Without a word the cross-eyed man arose and came down the room, one baleful eye fixed on William. He seized his victim by the neck and propelled him before him out of the room down the hall to the front door, where he ignominiously ejected him.

Ginger was anxiously awaiting his return.

"Hello," he greeted him, "you've not got it after all! Whatever's been happenin' in there?"

"All sorts of things," groaned William, rubbing his neck where the cross-eyed man had held it. "Crumbs! It was awful. They're havin' a meetin' an' it kept sayin' things an' they thought it was me. It was awful! An' he's nearly broke my neck."

"Where is it?" asked Ginger anxiously. He meant the parrot, not William's neck. He wasn't interested in William's neck.

"It went behind a sort of cupboard place," said William, still tenderly caressing his neck, "an' it was quite quiet till they started havin' a meetin' an' then it started sayin' its things an' they thought it was me. Crumbs! It was *awful!* . . . It's right behind the cupboard thing now. I kept tryin' to see it but I couldn't."

"Let's see if we can see it from the window," suggested Ginger.

They crept very, very cautiously up to the window. They could see the parrot quite plainly. It was on the floor behind the cupboard gazing about it with a sort of cynical enjoyment. It evidently had not spoken since it had secured William's ignominious ejection. It suddenly saw the Outlaws watching it through the window and began to walk towards them across the floor. So intent was the audience upon Miss Rubina Thomasina Fawshaw's discourse (she was giving a lucid account of the effect of alcohol upon the liver) that no one noticed the parrot walking sedately across the floor from the cabinet to the window. Having reached the window it stood for a few minutes gazing wickedly up at the Outlaws' faces. Then silently, suddenly it hopped up on to the open window sill. William put out his hand.

"Got it!" he breathed.

But he spoke too soon. He hadn't got it. With a chuckle it flew off over the fence into the next garden, leaving William and Ginger gazing after it despairingly.

"*Well!*" said William after an eloquent silence. "We seem sort of *doomed* with that bird!"

"Yes, an' if we've not got it put back by the time my aunt comes back we'll be still more doomed," said Ginger dejectedly.

"Come on then," said William, "let's catch it. It's only just sitting on a tree."

" Oh, shut up!" called the parrot, challengingly, from a small almond tree on which he was perching.

The two Outlaws scaled the fence and very, very

cautiously approached the truant.

"Got him *this* time," said William again joyfully as his outstretched hand descended.

But again he spoke too soon. The parrot squawked "Get out, you fool," and slipping nimbly away from William's grimy hand flew on to the window sill where it hopped up and down excitedly as if executing a war dance.

"Go on, Ginger," said William. "Get him! You can get him there all right!"

Ginger pounced desperately, but the parrot merely hopped through the open window into the front room of the house.

"*There!*" said William, hoarse with horror and despair, "it's gone into *another* house. Well, I've jolly well done enough goin' into houses after it an' getting pushed out with someone's fingers nearly meetin' through my neck. You can jolly well go after it, this time."

"A' right," said Ginger meekly, surveying the room with some anxiety.

"Go on—it's all right. It's empty 'cept for it," said William.

The parrot had perched upon an electric light that hung down from the centre of the ceiling and was swinging briskly to and fro. Ginger slowly pushed up the window and slung one leg over the ledge.

Then he looked back at William.

" 'S goin' to be an awful job catchin' him alone," he said pleadingly.

William had been regretting his decision not to join the expedition. William hated not being in the thick of an adventure.

"All right," he said, "I bet it will take both of us to catch him."

And despite his recent ignominious ejection he slung

his leg over the sill after Ginger with quite pleasurable feelings of zest and excitement.

The parrot had stopped swinging on the electric light bulb now and was hopping to and fro upon a polished table. He suggested someone slightly inebriated trying to perform a very complicated dance. He probably *was* slightly inebriated with freedom and excitement. . . . The two Outlaws approached him. With one beady eye fixed on them, but still merrily performing his dance, he waited again till Ginger's outstretched hand was a fraction of an inch from his back, and then with a diabolical chuckle he flew straight out of the window again.

"*Crumbs!*" said William. "Quick! Let's go after him or we shan't know which way he's gone."

But just at that minute there came the sound of the opening of a door and voices approached the room. Someone was coming. . . . There wasn't time to get out of the window. Already someone was holding the handle and the voices were just outside the door. Quick as lightning William and Ginger plunged beneath the nearest piece of furniture which happened to be a sofa with—mercifully—a frilled loose cover that hid them from view. There wasn't room to move or breathe but they felt grateful for the temporary shelter it afforded.

They were in fact so much exercised with the problem of existence in a space that did not allow for movement or breathing that at first they did not listen to what the voice were saying. But having partially solved the problem of existence in the cramped space and becoming gradually accustomed to the taste of the carpet their attention fixed itself upon the conversation that was going on in the room. Neither Ginger nor William could see the speakers, but the voices were those of a girl and a man. The girl was saying:

"Then we'll do Latham House on Wednesday?"

"I think so," said the man's voice.

"What time?"

"I suggest three o'clock. Will that do for you?"

"Yes, Quite well. You're *sure* they're away?"

"Oh, yes. . . . We can get the things ready in the coach-house. All the servants are away too."

"Good! I hope it will be a success. Frenshams' was a *great* success, wasn't it?"

They may have said more, but the Outlaws heard no more. They were dazed and astounded by the one stupendous fact. They had found the burglars. They swallowed several mouthfuls of carpet dust in sheer ecstasy. . . . They had found the burglars. Soon the closing of the door and the silence that followed it told them that the room was empty, and they crept out of their hiding-place, tiptoed across the room and clambered out of the still open window.

"Gosh!" said William as soon as they were outside. "The burglars!"

Ginger was no less thrilled than William, but the parrot still lay upon his conscience.

"The parrot!" he murmured, looking around at the parrotless expanse of sky and road and garden that met his gaze.

William looked about too. There was certainly no sign of the parrot.

"Oh, never mind the parrot!" he said contemptuously. "What's a *parrot?*"

Ginger murmured, truly enough, that a parrot is a parrot, but William stoutly denied it and even Ginger felt that a parrot paled into complete insignificance besides a burglar.

"She won't know it was us," said William (though without conviction), "and, anyway, it's lunch time. I'm *sick* of tryin' to catch parrots. Burglars are more fun and I bet they're a jolly sight easier to catch."

"What d'you think we'd better do?" said Ginger. "Go round to Latham House at three o'clock an' catch 'em?"

But even William's glorious optimism could not quite visualise this capture. He frowned for a minute perplexedly. Then he said:

"Tell you what! We'll get Robert to come an' help. He's mad keen on catchin' 'em."

"And Hector," said Ginger.

"All right," agreed William. "Robert an' Hector. We'll tell 'em after dinner—on condition that they let us help with the catchin'."

"Of course," said Ginger.

* * *

William found that there was no need to lead up to the question of the burglaries. Robert at lunch could talk of nothing else. He had decided quite definitely to capture the burglars. William knew that this decision was inspired solely by a desire to attain a heroic standard in the eyes of Miss Julia Bellairs. Robert wanted to catch the burglar not for the sake of the adventure but so that Miss Julia Bellairs might hear that he had caught the burglar. While despising the motive William appreciated the decision.

"My theory is," said Robert importantly, "that they'll do our house this afternoon. You see, they've probably discovered that we'll all going to be out this afternoon. They know that the maids are going to the fair at Balton and that I'm going out to the tennis club, and that you and Ethel are going to the Barlows' and William's going to tea to Ginger's. They always find out exactly which house is going to be empty during the afternoon. Now I've decided to pretend to go out to tennis, but I'm going to come back by the back way and wait in the house for them. They won't be expecting me, you see, and I'll overpower them before they've time to resist and——"

"How will you overpower them?" said Ethel, quite unimpressed.

"Well," said Robert still more importantly, "I know a very good way to do that. I was reading in the paper about a man who did it. He knew that a burglar was coming, so he arranged a pail of water over the back door, where he knew he'd come in because it was the only door not fastened and it fell down on him and drenched him and took away his breath, so that the man got him tied up before he recovered his breath."

"You mustn't do any such things, Robert," said Mrs. Brown indignantly, "*ruining* the carpets!"

William took no part in the discussion. William believed in doing one thing at a time and he was giving his whole attention to the Irish stew. Moreover, he realised that Robert must be approached privately, man to man, on the subject. Women had such queer ideas. Both his mother and his sister would, he knew, want to mess up the whole thing by bringing in the police.

So he followed Robert into the garden after lunch to impart his information.

"I say, Robert," he began carelessly. "I know all about those burglars. They aren't comin' here to-day. They're going' to Latham House. At three o'clock. I heard 'em say so."

"Rubbish!" said Robert with elder brother contempt and severity.

"*Honest,* Robert!" persisted William. "I'm not makin' it up. Honest, I'm not. Ask Ginger. We heard 'em talkin' when we was out this morning."

"Where did you hear them talking?" said Robert.

William hesitated. To answer that question accurately would be to reveal the whole parrot episode—an episode far better left unrevealed. Robert would have no compunction at all about informing Ginger's aunt that it had been Ginger and William who had let her parrot out. After a slight hesitation William replied unblushingly:

"Up on the common. On one of the seats."

He assuaged his conscience (that very amenable organ) firstly by the consideration that the story in the main was true and the details were unessential and secondly that probably all land was common land before they built houses on it, so really he wasn't telling a story at all.

"What were they saying?" said Robert with slightly less contempt and severity.

"Well, one of them was a woman and she said, 'Let's go an' burgle Latham House to-morrow,' an' they arranged to do that, an' they said that they knew that it would be empty an' they said they'd get their jemmies and things ready in the coach-house an' one of them said what a lot of fine things they got out of Frenshams'."

"Yes, they said that," said William vaguely, "at least, I *think* they said that. They said somethin' like it, anyway. About all the fine things they stole out of it."

"What were they like to look at?" said Robert.

William realised that if he'd heard them talking on a bench he must have seen them.

"Oh, they looked—they jus' looked like thieves," said William vaguely. "He'd got a beard an' she'd got black hair.

So plainly did William visualise the couple he described—a Russian communist and a vamp once seen on the pictures—that he could hardly believe he hadn't really seen them.

"She'd got a lot of jewellery on—things she'd stole, I suppose—an' he'd got a muffler half-way up his face an' cap pulled down low over his eyes."

"How did you know he'd got a beard then?" said Robert.

William was taken aback just for a second, but quickly recovered himself.

"It was one of those sorts of beards that stretch right up to the top of the person's face and then it went down underneath his muffler too. It was a big sort of beard."

"Did you say Ginger was with you?"

"Yes. We thought you an' Hector would like to catch 'em without troublin' the police."

"Oh, the police!" said Robert with a scornful laugh (Robert had been reading a good many detective stories lately). "The police aren't much good at anything like this. They muddle every case they touch. But," rather coldly, "I don't see why it was necessary to bring Hector into it. I could have managed it perfectly well without Hector."

"Well, nacherally," retorted William. "Ginger wanted to have Hector in it same as I wanted to have you in it. If we thought we could have done it ourselves we wouldn't have had either of you in it, but we thought that probably bein' bigger than what we are they'd overpower us before we'd time to catch 'em properly. But, anyway, Ginger heard it same as I did, an' he's as much right to have Hector in it as I have to have you."

"All right," said Robert stiffly, "I suppose it cannot be helped now, in any case. I suppose he'll have told him."

A month ago Robert would have delighted in having Hector to catch the thieves with him. A month ago Hector had been his bosom friend. But since a month ago they had both met Miss Julia Bellairs, and now Hector was no longer his bosom friend but his rival.

They gave each other now only the barest sign of recognition when meeting in the street, and when they were both in the presence of the beloved they affected to be unaware of each other's existence. . . . The one drawback in Robert's eyes to the present situation was that the glory of catching the thieves red-handed would have to be shared with Hector. Still, probably the beloved would understand that Hector had been merely Watson to his Sherlock Holmes. If she did not so understand Robert decided it should not be for lack of hints. . . . "A useful fellow, Hector," he would say, "of course, I couldn't have brought it off without him. I planned the whole thing, of course, but I couldn't have pulled it off without someone to help me."

"How're you goin' to catch 'em?" said William with interest.

Robert tore himself with an effort from a pleasant day dream in which Miss Julia Bellairs was saying, "But how *splendid!* How *wonderful!* How *brave!* . . . Weren't you afraid of being killed?"

And he was replying with a modest laugh: "Well, you know, I never thought of it. I never do when there's any danger."

"Er—you said three o'clock, didn't you?" he said coldly to William.

He wished he'd discovered the thing himself. It spoilt it somehow to have William and Ginger and Hector in it. . . .

"Yes," said William, "an' they were goin' to get their tools ready in the coach-house."

"Well," said Robert assuming a stern and superior air, as befitted a master detective, addressing one of his underlings, "I'll see Hector and tell him what to do."

* * *

They were all in the coach-house of Latham House. It was five minutes to three. Robert had fixed up a very complicated erection—consisting of a lot of ropes and a pail of water—over the door of the coach-house in such a way that anyone opening the door would receive the contents of the pail in full force upon their head. At least Robert hoped he would. His band of underlings had proved disappointingly unaccommodating about that. He had urged them—or one of them—to go out by the window and enter by the door in order to see whether the contrivance worked and all of them had refused. Robert rather hoped that Hector would offer. His pride as he gazed up at the elaborate erection was clouded only by the thought that no official of Scotland Yard would see it. He felt that if any official in Scotland Yard were to see it, they would at once offer him a high salaried post on the staff. Robert had often thought that he would make a good detective. . . .

Hector was bitterly resenting the airs that Robert was putting on over this. He was afraid that Miss Julia Bellairs would think that Robert's share in the capture was more important than it really was. He was indulging in a day dream in which the beloved was saying to him: "How *wonderful!* How *brave!* But weren't you *afraid?*"

And he was saying nonchalantly:

"Oh, no. Not a bit. I never am, you know. I'd really as soon have done it without Robert, but the poor boy was very anxious to help and I didn't like to refuse him."

"It's nearly three,' said William hopefully.

William was feeling that if he could just live to see that pail of water overturning on to somebody he didn't mind how soon he died after it.

"Quick," said Robert. "We'd better hide! They mustn't see us through the window."

"Hide quickly," said Hector, in order to prove to

himself that he was giving orders, not taking them from Robert.

They retired to the shadowy corner of the room—only just in time. Almost at once two figures were seen to pass the window walking furtively in single file. The windows were smeared and dusty, but it was clear that the figures were those of a man and a woman. They stopped at the door. Very cautiously they opened it and entered.

Robert's contrivance acted. It acted even more effectively than he had intended it to act. Not only did the bucket discharge its contents upon the couple as they entered. It discharged itself as well, completely enveloping both of them. The four amateur Sherlock Holmes' came out of their hiding-places to behold the amazing spectacle of two drenched forms—one a man and the other a woman—sitting back to back, the upper portion of both their forms completely enveloped by a tin bucket which had very neatly caught them both. Muffled screams and shouts came from beneath the bucket. With admirable presence of mind Robert darted forward and firmly held down the extinguisher.

"Get the rope quick, Hector," he said.

Even as he said it he was mentally composing an account of the affair for Miss Julia Bellairs.

"At once I held down the bucket quite firmly despite their struggling and called to Hector to get the rope for me to tie them up."

How he wished she were here to see him. . . .

The two were firmly bound together and then Robert with a flourish removed the extinguisher.

It revealed the bedraggled upper portions of Miss Julia Bellairs and her cousin.

There followed a scene that baffles description.

William and Ginger crept unostentatiously away

ROBERT, WITH A FLOURISH, REMOVED THE BUCKET.
"JULIA!" HE GASPED.

before it had even reached its climax, but before they departed they had gathered that Miss Julia Bellairs and her cousin were not burglars, but that they were engaged in the production of a little souvenir booklet of the village to be presented to every guest at a garden party they were giving the next month. The booklet was to contain a photograph of the house of every guest but this was to be a surprise—hence the mystery surrounding the taking of the photographs.

As William said: "With a cracked idea like that they couldn't *expect* anythin' but trouble."

* * *

It was that evening.

William and Ginger walked slowly and sadly down the road.

"Then there's that parrot," said Ginger gloomily.

"Yes. I'd been quite forgetting the parrot," said William.

"It started it all," said Ginger yet more gloomily.

"I s'pose so," said William, "but she doesn't know you let it out. She's not been to see your father about it yet, has she?"

"No, but she might any time—an' on the top of the *other*——"

"Let's g'n' see what she's doin' about it," said William, who never could resist the temptation to revisit the scene of a crime.

They approached Ginger's aunt's house and once more crept cautiously up to the drawing-room window.

The first sight that met their eyes was the reassuring one of Ginger's Aunt's parrot hanging as usual in the cage and swinging to and fro on his perch.

Further investigation revealed the figure of Ginger's aunt and a friend sitting over a tea table.

Their conversation reached the watchers through the open window.

"Oh, yes, he's a *very* clever bird," Ginger's aunt was saying proudly. "Why, do you know what he did this morning? Some one must have left the window open and he opened his cage door *himself* and got out. Right out of the window. I was *distracted* when I came home and found him gone. And then just when I was in the middle of ringing up the police about it he came back. Simply came in again through the window and went back into his cage."

The two Outlaws crept back to the road.

"Well, *that's* all right!" said William.

"Yes," admitted Ginger, "that's cert'nly *one* thing all right. . . . What're you goin' to do now?"

"I'm not quite sure," said William. "Only," very firmly. "I'm not goin' home jus' yet. Robert's goin' out at six o'clock an' I'm not goin' home till after that."

"I'm not either," said Ginger. "Hector's goin' out about then an' I'm not goin' home till after that . . . you'd think they'd be grateful to us, wouldn't you? It made them friends again."

"Yes, but they aren't grateful to us," said William, "and, of course, it made Robert madder still to find that the burglars had been to our house while he'd been out tryin' to catch 'em at Latham House."

"Yes, and the way they make it all out *our* fault——" said Ginger bitterly.

"They always do that," said William.

"She said she'd never speak to 'em again," said Ginger meditatively, "but she said some jolly fine things to 'em first. Before she said that."

"So did he," said William.

With reminiscent appreciative smiles on their countenances they walked on slowly down the road.

THE END